My Favorite Lies

My Favorite Lies

Stories by
Ruth Hamel

University of Missouri Press
Columbia and London

Copyright © 2001 by Ruth Hamel
University of Missouri Press, Columbia, Missouri 65201
Printed and bound in the United States of America
All rights reserved
5 4 3 2 1   05 04 03 02 01

Library of Congress Cataloging-in-Publication Data
Hamel, Ruth, 1958-
    My favorite lies : stories / by Ruth Hamel.
        pm. cm.
    ISBN 0-8262-1356-1 (alk. paper)
        1. United States–Social life and customs–20th century–Fiction.
            I. Title.

PS3608.A55 M9 2001
813'.6–dc21

                                        2001041599

Design and composition: Vickie Kersey DuBois
Printer and binder: The Maple-Vail Book Manufacturing Group
Typefaces: Claustrum, Palatino, Shelly Allegro Script

For Tim

Contents

Acknowledgments

Some of the stories in this collection appeared in the following publications: "My Favorite Lies," *Prairie Schooner;* "Myra," *The Kenyon Review;* "Good Girl," *New Orleans Review;* "Go," *North American Review;* "These Things," *Folio;* "The Years in Review," *Ascent;* "Careful," *The Missouri Review;* "Everglade," *The Hartford Advocate;* "I'll Hold You Up," *Provincetown Arts.*

I don't like to consider what these stories would be without the help they received from a large, far-flung group of readers, including (but by no means limited to) Jeff Bens, Portia Bohn, Catherine Brady, Greg Collins, Marko Fong, Elena Gorokova, Patricia Hackbarth, Zdena Heller, LeVell Holmes, Tom Jones, Elisabeth Jones, Steven Kahn, Ruthanne Lum McCunn, Henry Meyerson, Mildred Verba Morris, Mark Ong, Judith Peck, Sally Rosenbluth, Emily Russell, Ruth Sasaki, Pearl Canick Solomon, William Warner, and Stan Yogi.

Then there's the help *I* have received, in the form of patient encouragement from friends who understand that I can only take so much honesty. Several names on the previous list also fall into this category, but one person must be singled out: Jeff Levine. He knows why.

Finally, my husband, Tim Schreiner, has provided generous support of several varieties and displayed heroic endurance in the face of relentless whining and hand-wringing.

My Favorite Lies

Kinded

Roger's bridge toll had already been paid.

"The Beemer got you."

"Pardon?"

The woman in the tollbooth jabbed her thumb over her shoulder, at the licorice-black BMW convertible that had preceded Roger through the gate and now was darting through the city-bound traffic on the bridge. "The Beemer paid for you."

Roger squinted up at her. It was seven in the morning, the April sky was gray and crumpled, and she was the first person he'd spoken to since leaving the office twelve hours before.

"You've been kinded," the woman said, enunciating with sarcastic precision. Her earrings, brass hearts, jerked in disdain. "I'll be glad when this bullshit runs its course."

"I guess," Roger said. As he pulled onto the deck of the bridge, he looked for the BMW, but his benefactor was long gone.

Guerrilla acts of charity had lately become the rage. Roger had read about it in the newspaper, how a few bumper stickers encouraging "random kindness and senseless acts of beauty" had started a movement, or at least a fad, inspiring people to buy roses for beggar women and slip coins into strangers' parking meters. You never knew when you'd be singled out, according to the paper, but Roger was surprised that one of these gestures had been aimed at him. He knew he didn't look poor—had he looked sick or maybe unhappy? He was even more perplexed by the source of the good deed: The BMW had been smugly overpolished, with license plates that proclaimed its owner an ARTSNOB. Crawling through the tollbooth line behind the vulgar car, Roger had speculated at length about the invisible driver's vanities and foibles. Then kindness had caught him up short.

1

Halfway across the bridge he realized that he should have passed on the favor and paid the toll for the car behind him. It probably had been expected of him.

Roger's lapse preoccupied him all the way to the office. He decided to repay the charity that evening on his trip back through the toll lanes. In the meantime, he couldn't wait to tell Margaret what had happened. But when he got to work, kindness and its attendant irritations were swept aside. A snake was waiting on his desk.

Technically, it was a belt. Not a snakeskin belt, but a whole snake, split and dried, white stripes on black, with a fanged silver buckle where the real head used to be.

Roger said, "I'm afraid of snakes."

"I know."

"Ever since I was a kid. That's why he sent it." Margaret sat on the other side of his desk, weighing the gift on her upturned palms. The very sight of it made Roger's scalp crawl backward. "But the belt's not even the worst thing."

"What's the worst thing?" She asked this in the singsong voice she used to humor him.

"He's coming to visit."

"When?"

Roger waved the note. "He only said he was on his way. He'll just show up here—today, for all I know—expecting me to drop everything and meet him."

"How long since you've seen him?"

"Three years? Four."

Margaret dispensed one eloquent blink: *But he's your brother.*

Roger considered Margaret his best friend. He freely told her about each fresh romantic mishap and professional faux pas, about his ragged nerves, bad dreams, selfish impulses, and frequently chafed conscience, but he'd never told her much about his brother. Margaret was a compact, orderly person; from her hair to her clothes, nothing hung loose. She had a social worker girlfriend, an honor roll daughter, and a registered schnauzer, and they all lived happily in a house without a junk drawer. How could she understand Chase, who claimed that he'd never passed a peaceful night and never once been loved?

"Here." She tried to hand the belt to Roger; he drew back, raising his palms like a hold-up victim. She set it on his desk. "The Pratt people are coming in at nine. Are we ready?"

"Almost." There was no time to tell her about the BMW. Maybe after the meeting. He knew what she would say— "Any sort of kindness should be cherished these days, shouldn't it?"—but he needed to hear it just the same.

For twelve years Roger and Margaret had worked side by side in a one-room office, writing and designing annual reports for other companies; they were experts at putting a good public face on disappointing results. For twelve years Margaret had been trying to get Roger to relax, and he had relied upon her to assure him that despite everything—his nerves, conscience, what have you—despite all that, he was more or less OK.

"Margaret?" He pointed to the snake on his desk. "Will you put this somewhere? I can't touch it."

Twining around jungle branches; swaying, charmed, to a Calcutta flute; springing from the chaparral to make the horses scream—

Snakes would not let Roger be. When he was a child, they had writhed all around him, in classroom filmstrips and matinee Westerns and his family's large, soft lawn. The ones he'd imagined were worse: slithering under the bedsheets and through the walls, unstoppable. Even now, at forty-seven, he confronted at least one snake a week, on late-night TV or in magazine ads. Once, waiting to cross the street, he realized that the jaunty young man beside him was wearing a python like a scarf. The snake was near enough to dart its head and kiss Roger's cheek; although he'd been too shocked to feel fear at that moment, the memory pounced again and again, always when he was on the verge of sleep, forcing him to reach preemptively for his strongest pills.

Chase's belt wasn't all that surprising. He liked to give aggressive presents. Once he'd sent Roger a bear rug complete with
claws and shellacked yellow teeth; it had been too long for the
living room floor and spent a week with its neck bent back, staring glumly at the apartment ceiling, until Roger took pity on it,
rolled it up, and dragged it down to the street. On Roger's forti-
eth birthday he came home from work to find an empty, molder-
ing steamer trunk waiting outside his door. Since then, Chase's
gifts had been less extravagant: a scorpion paperweight, a
bleached coyote skull. Money was tight, he said.

Chase was a paralegal and always managed to find work, but
he couldn't stay put. From Toledo to Eugene, no place he tried
was right. Some were too hot, some too windy. Some were
spoiled by rednecks, others overrun by foreigners. Roger no
longer bothered updating his address book, just jotted Chase's
new phone number on the nearest scrap and tried not to lose it.
Really, though, it was always his brother who made the calls,
unfailingly, on Christmas Eve, Memorial Day, and Roger's birthday. Each call began with the same question: "How's Big
Brother?"

"Oh, fine," Roger would reply.

There would be a pause. "Don't you want to know how I am?"

"Of course I do," Roger would say, though he didn't need to
ask. Then he would sit back for an hour, pinching his eyebrows,
praying for patience, trying not to listen too closely as his brother's misery poured over him.

When Roger got to the tollbooth that evening, six dollars in
hand, prepared to settle his random-kindness account, he
looked in his rearview mirror and saw the same car that had
tried to cut him off a few miles back. The neckless, bully-faced
driver was shouting into a cell phone. Roger decided to save his
good deed until the next day. But in the morning when he again
found himself facing the tolltaker with the brass-heart earrings,
he was afraid of aggravating her with another act of charity. He
resolved to give three dollars to the first homeless person he

saw. Once downtown, though, he found that the streets had been cleared of shopping carts and bedrolls. For weeks the mayor had been threatening to sweep the beggars away. Roger was surprised by how empty the city felt without them. Where had they been banished to? Where did you put people when you finally got fed up?

Not far from his office, Roger saw a man about his age aimlessly slouched on a corner. His jeans were dirty, and one of his bootlaces was broken. "Here you go," Roger said, holding out three dollars. "Buy yourself some shoelaces." Too late, he noticed the bus stop sign. "Shit. I mean, I'm sorry."

The man recoiled, holding up his metal lunchbox as if it could shield him from Roger. A bus pulled up, plastered with an ad featuring breath mints and a boa constrictor.

No sooner had Roger finished reporting this episode to Margaret—laughing, but wanting to talk it away—than his phone rang.

"How's Big Brother?"

"Chase."

"Guess where I am." The voice was so close it might have been speaking from between Roger's ears.

"Right downstairs, I'll bet."

"Two blocks away. What are you doing?"

"Actually, I'm just going into a meeting. Can we get together later?"

"I'm busy later."

Roger was certain that Chase knew no one else in the city; he decided to call his bluff. "I guess we'll have to get together tomorrow, then." But he knew he should invite Chase to spend the night in his spare room. Sitting at her desk with her back to him, Margaret was too motionless to be doing anything but eavesdropping. "Do you have a place to stay tonight?"

A sigh. A pause. Then, flatly, "I think I've got it covered."

This was Roger's cue to beg, but the old barricades were dropping into place. "All right. Tomorrow then. I'll take you to lunch."

After hanging up, he looked reflexively toward Margaret. "He wanted me to make him mad, so he could be mad at me." Over the years Roger had gotten used to addressing the back of her head. "And it's not just me. He can't get along with anybody." Doubtfully, she blinked at him in the mirror over her desk. "I mean it. Take him to a baseball game and the beer vendor is ignoring him. Go to the supermarket, the bagger is deliberately bruising his fruit. The world is one big asshole."

Margaret twirled her chair around. "Is he married?"

"Never. And he never will." Roger hadn't married either, but he still dated.

"You don't talk about him," Margaret said. "Is he . . . ?" She drummed her fingertips on her brow.

"No. But he's not exactly right."

"Well. Who is?"

Roger refused to return her smile. Sometimes Margaret's relentless equanimity could be irritating—showy, like dropping names or tailgating in an expensive car. He said, "Chase won't even try to act like a normal person."

"Maybe it's not that easy."

"I do it. Mercy, look at these numbers." The latest financial results for Pratt Industries were spread across his desk. The worst yet.

Margaret reluctantly turned back to her work. Roger gathered the Pratt numbers into a stack. He really didn't want to discuss Chase. He wasn't sure why; he told her everything else. But it hurt to talk about his brother. It was like coughing up stones.

Roger studied Pratt's lackluster earnings, trying to work up phrases that would soothe the stockholders. *Resisting the lure of short-term profits . . . investing in a vibrant future.* But he'd used almost the same words last year. Had anyone ever been fooled? He pinched his eyebrows. *I am not my brother.* These words, both reminder and prayer, had sustained him many times. He picked up a highlighting pen and scoured the Pratt numbers for anything that could be twisted into hope. He got up for a copy of last year's report. He clipped a hangnail. Then he pushed Pratt's troubles aside and waited for Margaret to ask him what was wrong so that he could tell her about his brother.

Chase remembered everything. Well, everything bad. Nothing good had managed to stick to his flystrip memory. Roger could picture it: a gluey corkscrew curl encrusted with black betrayals, insults, and disappointments, dangling in the center of his brother's airless head, undisturbed by breezy joys or bright surprises. Every rude boss. Every forsaking woman. Every stolen parking place and dirty restaurant fork. Every misstep their parents had taken.

Traying last year's Pratt report, Roger tried to explain his family to Margaret: Their father traveled a lot. Their mother stayed inside. Chase was difficult; Roger, high-strung. They lived in a nice house on a good street, but somehow it was understood that life had not turned out well for them. Still, the family continued as families once had, until the father's heart quit and the sons moved away and the mother slowly died. The house was sold to another family that undoubtedly had problems of its own. What more was there to say?

Sometimes Roger heard Chase's complaints out in silence; other times he had to scold. "You're forty-four years old, and they're both dead, and they weren't even that bad—"

"If that's what you want to believe."

"What did they do so wrong? How were they so much worse than anyone else?"

Chase would then set out a sampler of pungent memories: the Christmas their father didn't come home, the week their mother stopped talking.

"He was snowed in at O'Hare," Roger argued. "And she had a terrible migraine. I remember things a lot differently."

"Fine, if it helps you sleep at night."

This was the most infuriating insinuation Chase could make—that he was forced to stand guard over the past, an exhausted but vigilant sentry, while Roger snored blithely on. He always managed to imply that his own joyless life was the proper one to lead and Roger's the dishonest, shameful one. So Roger would lose patience and tell Chase to stop looking backward, and Chase would hang up, insulted, and they wouldn't speak until the next Christmas Eve, Memorial Day, or birthday.

"He's grateful for nothing," Roger told Margaret. "Not sunshine, not good health, not being alive."

"Maybe you should just be glad you aren't him," Margaret said. "Imagine what it's like."

"No."

"You can't?"

"I won't." Sometimes before sleep Roger's wandering brain would do just that, brush up against his brother's life, but he always managed to stop and back away, quickly, before pity could pounce and pin him down.

Chase had no one to blame but himself. Hadn't Roger managed to make a life? He'd stayed in the same city for fifteen years. He owned his apartment. He had interests and still hoped to find someone. He tried to harvest what happiness he could.

Usually, he liked the tidy office he shared with Margaret, but that day it seemed cramped and dim. He decided to go out to lunch; he craved light and air and strangers, even though he risked running into Chase. When he stepped outside, he almost laughed from surprise and delight. After a week of drooping gray skies, the clouds were burning away. Roger could never quite remember that clear sky backed the clouds, not vice versa.

Lunch was fast and furtive, but he finally managed to repay the tollbooth charity, giving three dollars to a woman who was too drunk to notice. She was sitting on the sidewalk with her chin on her chest, drooling, maybe weeping; it was hard to tell. Roger wedged the money in her torn sleeve. Kindness was now off his back. He didn't feel much better.

At noon the next day, Roger was waiting in the lobby of his office building with his fist on his hip, pushing back his jacket to show off the snake belt. It looked ridiculous with his gray flannel slacks, and he shuddered whenever he touched it, but he was determined to show Chase that the belt didn't intimidate him.

Scanning the sidewalk crowd, searching for the familiar face, Roger resolved to act kindly toward his brother. He would offer helpful suggestions when appropriate and try to demonstrate the benefits of an optimistic outlook, and with any luck Chase would hit the road after lunch. Roger was exhausted, shaky after a night of prickling pillows and twisted bedsheets, so worn down by sleeplessness that it took him a moment to realize that Chase was there, standing in the middle of the sidewalk, staring at him through the lobby doors. He was wearing running shoes and a heavy raincoat, and he was making people step around him.

Roger walked out and clapped his shoulder. "You could have come in, you know." Chase shrugged upward into Roger's palm. It was hard to tell whether he was prolonging the touch or casting it off.

Four years ago, tilting at the edge of their mother's grave, Chase had still looked like a young man, eager and raw, maybe a little too nerved-up but taut with life. Now crevices ran from his cheekbones to his jaw, and each eye sat in a saddle of crumpled gray flesh. His hair had tarnished and he wore it long, swept back behind his ears and down his neck. The effect was at once vainglorious and seedy.

Roger stared at him, speared by two thoughts. *No matter what else he exaggerates, he really is miserable.* Then, a split-second later, glancing away: *Why won't he help himself?*

"So," Roger said. "Four years."

"It looks like they've been good to you." Chase tugged on his watchband. "Five."

"What?"

"That's how long it's been. I was in Sacramento when she died. That was five years ago."

"You're right." Roger sighed, grateful to believe that the dead were really dead and not eavesdropping. He took hold of Chase's arm and pulled him out of the path of a skating messenger. "Do you want to walk around a little? Then we'll get something to eat."

He wasn't quite ready to sit down across from Chase. And it was a rare afternoon, warm and sharply lighted, with a confiding, nudging breeze. Everyone on the street seemed to be happy: executives, bureaucrats, truck drivers, winos, all of them surely bearing their own sorrows but able to put them aside for a little while to feast upon the day. Roger wanted to point this out to Chase, that other people tried to glean what joy they could. But he'd promised himself not to preach.

Chase moved slowly, gingerly, as if recovering from surgery. He kept his lips pressed in upon themselves, like a scolded child or a very old man. Roger knew he should be making conversation, but it was hard to talk over the traffic, and he didn't know where to begin. Everything he thought to say sounded phony. Finally, after they'd turned down a quieter block, he said, "You know you could have stayed with me."

"What?" Chase cupped his ear like a geezer. Forty-four years old.

"I said you could have stayed with me last night."

"I still wouldn't have slept. I can't, anymore."

Roger's phone rang, vibrating inside his jacket. He knew it was Margaret, calling to invite him and Chase to dinner. She'd mentioned it that morning as she helped him put on the belt, and he'd pretended not to hear her. He let it ring.

"Hey!" Chase's frown fell away. "You got my present."

Roger held open his jacket to show off the snake. "I meant to thank you yesterday."

"I got it at an Indian reservation. It's not exactly endangered, but they're hard to catch."

"Catch?" Roger laughed.

"OK, kill. Since when are you a stickler for the truth, Mr. Soft Soap?" This featherweight insult had a liberating effect. Chase began to walk faster, keeping up with everyone else, twirling his raincoat belt in one hand. He began to talk.

He was passing through the city on his way to Portland, Maine. He'd given up on the raw West; he needed a change of light and history. This time he would look for something different to do. "The problem with paralegal work is that some of these cases never end. I just spent a year on an asbestos suit, and it could drag on for five more. Mercy, look at this."

They were approaching the woman who'd won Roger's random kindness the day before, still sitting on the sidewalk but with a pink prosthetic leg propped beside her real, bruised calves. "You poor critter," Chase said. She patted the fake limb and held out her hand. Chase gave her two quarters. Roger gave her thirty cents. "I gave her three dollars yesterday," he explained.

"Three bucks!"

"A waste, I know. I'll tell you the whole story over lunch." He was ready now. "What do you feel like? Thai? Mexican?"

Chase grimaced. "I'm not that hungry. But there's a coffee shop at the hotel, if that's good enough."

"Fine," Roger said, borrowing the hearty tone he used with clients.

Roger had passed the Clearview many times without paying much attention. From the street it looked like an average tourist hotel. But as he followed Chase through the lobby, Roger saw that although the Clearview appeared to be clean and safe, it did not provide the slightest human comfort. The lobby had no carpets or plants or music, just square-edged vinyl sofas and overhead fluorescent rings. The desk clerk worked behind a Plexiglas shield. Somewhere a drill was screeching.

Roger and Chase were the only customers in the luncheonette and quickly ran afoul of the waitress, an older woman with a Christian fish pin and a carved-in sneer that deepened with each request they made (a brighter booth, a clean knife, water for Roger's aspirin). Chase kept a wary eye upon her as she moved about the restaurant.

Indoors, his brother looked even more exhausted, weary beyond the help of sleep. His leather watchband was cinched tight, and he kept touching it as if it hurt him. But he spoke hopefully about his new life in Portland. Every so often he would glance down at Roger's belt and smile to himself.

"So tell me why you gave that drunk three dollars."

"Random kindness." Roger tried to explain—the BMW at the tollbooth, the man at the bus stop, the whole sorry slapstick of charity. "It was awful how I had to get it off my back."

"Like you were cursed."

"Exactly. *Kinded*."

Chase was grinning, deeply tickled. Really, Roger thought, this wasn't so bad. They might have been any two brothers sharing lunch. The phone rang again, chirping inside his jacket. He ignored it. Margaret was only trying to be nice, but dinner was out of the question.

The waitress set down their food grudgingly, as if they were beggars who should not be encouraged. Chase tasted his soup, dropped his spoon, and groped around the table with impatient hands. He raised one arm above his head, snapped his fingers, and bellowed. "Salt! We need salt here!"

The waitress hesitated just long enough to register her contempt before she returned to the table. With ostentatious precision she set down a hefty plastic shaker. "Thank you," Roger said.

When Chase picked up the shaker and tipped it over his soup, the lid dropped off, sending a cascade of salt into his bowl.

"Mercy," Roger said.

Chase stared down at his ruined lunch.

"I guess it's lucky you weren't hungry," Roger said. "Hang on." He waved for the waitress, who smiled as she carried the bowl away.

"It was an accident," Roger said.

Chase clamped his lips together. When the woman brought him a fresh bowl of soup, he pushed it aside. "They're going to charge you double."

Roger knew it was pointless to attempt verbal consolation. He decided to make a show of enjoying his own lunch. His grilled cheese sandwich was burned around the edges, cold and rubbery in the center, just like their mother used to make, though he was not about to mention it. He wanted to talk about the future, Portland and so forth. Odd how Chase could still summon up hope for a new place. At least the sandwich gave Roger an excuse to look down. It hurt to see his brother head-on; it always had.

Chase tapped his water glass with his knife, as if about to propose a toast. "You should know I just had a bad scare. Healthwise."

Roger set down his sandwich. This was sure to be unappetizing.

"A polyp." He pronounced the word with relish.

Roger laid his paper napkin over his plate. "Those are pretty common, aren't they?"

"Common? I wouldn't say that."

"I mean, they're usually nothing."

"You never know." Chase tugged on his watchband, primly offended.

"But you're OK?"

He shrugged. Roger felt exasperation begin its familiar slow burn behind his ribs. A polyp! Everybody got those, didn't they? This was just like Chase, making the worst of everything, shamelessly cadging for pity. Roger could feel something else, a cold sort of pressure, building beneath his annoyance. "*Are* you OK?"

"That's what they say."

"They wouldn't lie, would they?"

"I don't mind telling you, I was scared." Chase leaned closer to Roger. "That it was all over."

"But it's not. So you should be happy, right?"

Chase rolled his eyes toward the ceiling. Roger took out his wallet, checked the bill. Indeed, the waitress had charged him twice for the soup.

"I can pay for me," Chase said.

"Not at all. Consider yourself kinded. Now, I'd better get back for my two o'clock. Maybe tomorrow we can—"

Chase reached across the table and took hold of Roger's wrist.

"You have to see my room."

Roger expected plain beige paint and a bolted-down TV. He got himself and Chase, reflected on every side. The walls were covered in mirrors.

"I knew you had to see it for yourself," Chase said. "You wouldn't have believed me otherwise."

They'd put him in an L-shaped room with a narrow window, a single bed, a picture of a polar bear, a small table, and one metal chair. Roger walked around, pressing on the glassy walls, surprised by how close they really were.

Chase sat on the bed, gestured toward the chair. "Take a seat."

"I have a two o'clock. Anyway, I don't mind standing." The window looked across an alley into an identical room with nobody in it. "So. When are you due in Portland?"

"You mean, when am I leaving."

"That wasn't—" But it was.

"Soon."

Guiltily, Roger sat on the hard little chair, directly across from Chase and a reflection of his own strained face. A vacuum cleaner was wailing in the next room. Doors were slamming up and down the hall.

Roger said, "It's no wonder you can't sleep, with all this racket."

Chase smiled and nodded, as if accepting a compliment. "What about you? Are you sleeping OK?"

"With the right pills." This was more than Roger normally would have admitted, but a memory had just caught him up short: Chase, stretched out on his back in his pajamas, clamping a pillow over his own face, trying to make himself sleep. Nine years old.

As memories went, this wasn't so bad. But Roger hadn't thought of it in many years and was startled by its sharpness. Most of Roger's memories were broken in and easy to handle.

A heavy door banged, again and again, rattling the mirrors. Two men began shouting in German. Chase sat on the edge of the gray bedspread with his hands folded on his knees.

Roger pinched his forehead and closed his eyes. "This is a terrible place." But he felt he was admitting something he shouldn't.

"It is," Chase said.

The vacuum cleaner thumped and shrieked on the other side of the wall. The phone in Roger's pocket was buzzing against his heart. He pressed his fingertips to his eyelids. The cold pressure was building, expanding like freezing water; he didn't know if it came from inside or out. He said, "You should stay with me tonight."

Chase didn't answer.

"It's quiet in my building. You can rest." Silence. Roger felt the afternoon's frustration gathering, but he surrendered a little bit more. "You can talk."

"Talk?"

"As much as you want."

"And you'll listen?"

"Have I ever had a choice?" Roger closed his eyes and waited for the familiar avalanche of accusation.

Chase softly tapped on the mirror beside the bed. "Look."

Roger didn't need to see. He already knew. They were brothers. His clothes cost more, Chase's wear and tear was more pronounced, but they shared the apprehensive hunch of their shoulders, the nervous fingers and knees, the insomniac bruises under their eyes.

Difficult. High-strung.

Roger knew this; it didn't matter. Only one thing mattered. "You don't have to stay here." He opened his eyes. "You don't have to live like this."

"I can stand it." Chase smiled, victorious.

Roger looked at his brother's exhausted face, and the pressure that had been building for an hour took shape as a thought too true to leave unspoken.

"Life was wasted on you."

Going home that evening, Roger paid two extra tolls, let three cars cut in front of him and bought a carnation from a deaf man at a stop light, but still found himself sleepless at midnight. He didn't bother with his pills. They never helped when he got like this. All he could do was twist up in his bedsheets, winding them about himself like a tourniquet. All he could do was let his mind gallop, rear, and trample for as long as it needed, within specific, fenced-off pastures.

First, anger. At Chase. At himself, of course, for saying what he had about wasted life (but it was true, wasn't it?). At the random-kindness people for their childish game, which had nothing to do with mercy. He even let himself be angry with Margaret, for her pushy hospitality and her ignorance. Tomorrow he would tell her: Some pain could not be helped by common sense and positive thinking.

Anger was quickly stamped down and kicked aside.

Next, Roger allowed his mind a leisurely graze upon guilt. It was a familiar feeling; he knew its twists and turns and barely paid attention as the memories unfurled. In one, his teenage self walked past Chase's open bedroom door and saw his brother sitting on his bed, not doing anything, just looking back at him. Roger was on his way out of the house, to a movie or game, but he made himself go in and talk to Chase. What did they talk about? That much was gone or buried.

Now it was time to sleep. Roger closed his eyes and concentrated on the tuneless hum of his building. There were thirty floors of people, but they were quiet, petless people, and outside there was a guarded gate to keep out vagrants and through-traffic. Roger had chosen this building with an eye to sound sleep, and most nights he managed tolerably well. Chase could have rested here too.

They needed quiet; they'd grown up in it. The house had been thickly carpeted and curtained, the neighborhood muffled by deep lawns and heavy trees. On the long summer Sundays, banished from the house, Roger and Chase would try to noiselessly amuse themselves. They'd lie flat on the grass, trying to feel the earth turn, trying not to quarrel. They knew the afternoon would be long, with their mother resting and their father far away.

Roger normally didn't let his mind roam about like this, but that night his bones ached from exhaustion and he could feel the current pulling at him, memory deep and swift. Maybe he'd be carried off to sleep.

Once they were playing Monopoly in the hot sun of the front lawn. Roger was eleven, Chase eight; Roger always the race car, Chase always the flat iron. They got into an argument about mortgages, and Chase hurled Roger's car into the hedge under the picture window. Roger was on his knees groping for the tiny piece when he saw a knot of snakes, five or six of them, tangled up to sun themselves in the hedge, just a few inches from his face.

He scrambled backward, squeaking. He'd always been afraid of snakes but had almost never seen them in real life. These were only garter snakes, not very big but horribly twisted together.

He called for Chase, who rushed forward to see. "I'm going to get Mom," Roger said, although he did not like to bother her. By the time she'd changed out of her bathrobe and ventured outdoors, Chase had alerted the neighbors. Women from the other houses were gathering to see the snakes.

"Roger, come out!" Chase kept calling to him, but Roger stayed indoors, looking out through the big living-room window. Just below him he could see Chase's round, buzz-cut head peering at the snakes; he could see his mother standing a little apart from the neighbor women. She was taller and skinnier than the others, and when they spoke to her she smiled tightly and bunched her daisy-printed skirt in her hands.

Suddenly, the women drew back, exclaiming in disgust. Chase was reaching into the hedge. He plucked out one snake, casually, like pulling a sock from a drawer, and draped it around his brown neck. He had taken off his shirt.

Roger tried to prod his mind toward another pasture, Pratt Industries, but Chase was shouting to him through the window.

"You have to see this!"

Roger crept as far as the front steps but could not make himself get any closer. The snake was winding over his brother's neck and chest and arms, and he could see that Chase was happy, thrilled by the slithering caress, proud of his own nerve. The neighborhood women were cringing and squealing, and Roger's mother was shaking her head in mock exasperation. Chase said, "Mom, it feels good," and Roger could hear the women's laughter sharpen. "That's enough," his mother said. Chase hunched over to let the snake crawl over his bare back. "I said, stop." She stepped toward him, and Roger knew that she wanted to pull his arm or yank his hair, but she didn't dare, afraid of the women or maybe the snake. The cords on her throat stuck out; her pale lips pressed in upon themselves. "No wonder the kids don't want to play with you," she said.

Her voice came out too raw, too young. Chase straightened up, letting the snake fall to the grass. Squinting, as if perhaps he hadn't heard right, then crossing his arms over his bare chest.

"And you." She turned to Roger. "What's going to happen to you? You're too old to be scared."

"You're scared," he said. "You're always scared."

Inside, she would have done something. Inside, he never would have said it. But they were outside, and she could only stand crumpling her skirt in her hands, her eyes shining with defeat and helplessness, just as Chase had looked at her a moment before. And Roger could step away from both of them. He walked through the ring of neighbor women, down the driveway, down the sidewalk, knowing that they would not dare to follow him. At the corner he glanced back: The women had gone, but his mother and Chase were still watching him, standing side by side on the rolling lawn, Chase skinny and half-naked, his mother twisting her arms behind her back. They each called Roger's name once before he turned and walked out of sight.

When their father got home, he took the boys out for surf and turf, like clients. "Roger," he said, cracking a claw, "maybe it's not a good idea for you to talk to your mother." Then, "Chase, maybe you could try a little harder to make her happy."

As bad memories went, this wasn't much. Other people, even Margaret, had much worse things in storage. Roger let the bedsheet loosen, just a little, and tried to listen to his building's tranquilizing hum. He would sleep now, but first he allowed himself one sip of pity, for his mother. When she finally was left alone to embark upon her long wasting, it was like a trip she'd been waiting to take her whole life.

Roger slowly relaxed into a browsing kind of sorrow, wandering through rooms of sad but familiar memories. His father, calling home, always identifying himself: "Roger, this is your dad." Dying in the hotel elevator, suitcase by his side, discovered by a janitor.

His mother, pulling the curtains shut. Fixing him a sandwich, half-burned, half-cold, then sitting to watch him eat. Straining toward him, wanting something, unable to say what. It was terrible to see; he'd kept his eyes on his food.

Chase, walking home alone from school. Crossing the stage to receive his high school diploma, walking so stiffly, frowning so stubbornly, that people in the audience had burst out laughing.

Roger pictured himself, neatly dressed but very small, tiptoe-ing past each of these rooms and softly closing their doors.

Suddenly, he understood, in every cell of his heart, that the waitress at the Clearview had loosened the top of the salt shak-er, had deliberately ruined Chase's lunch. That was his brother's life. People insulted and aggravated him for the sheer sport of it. Roger had always known this on some level. Now he felt it from the inside out; he was there with Chase, in Eureka and Tucson and Wichita, emptying the cupboards, packing the soft, battered boxes, surrendering one more time.

Roger rolled in the bedsheet, tightening the cloth until he was swaddled and bound, with his cold feet protruding from one end and his hot, rumpled head from the other. Grief was roast-ing him alive, from the inside. Grief, and something else, which he didn't have a word for. It felt nothing like pity, nothing like guilt; it was stronger, unstoppable, roaring through him, burn-ing down the barricades, making a hole for the world to crowd into: the drunk with the fake leg, the man with the bootlace, the toll taker, old girlfriends and neighbors and relatives, even Margaret, all pressing together, filling him up, crying, "Feel me! Be me!" And he could, he had no choice, but there was nothing kind or beautiful about it. He was only a raw heart, tired and poor, too weak to help anyone else.

But he finally fell asleep.

When the alarm rang, Roger was still loosely wrapped in his bandage of sheet. He didn't want to get up and face the city; he couldn't stand to see one more broken person. But he had a nine o'clock meeting with Pratt and, before that, breakfast with his brother. He got up, washed himself, and strapped on the snake belt once more.

Chase's hard-shelled gray suitcase was packed and waiting by the door of the L-shaped room. Roger squinted at it. "Isn't that—"

"Dad's. It's really lasted."

Roger had intended to offer cappuccino and a drive through the historic district, but once inside the room he saw that Chase had gotten hold of a second chair and a pot of room-service coffee. So he sat. He made himself listen. It hurt, but no worse than he'd hurt the night before, all by himself.

Finally, it was time to leave. He had one question for Chase. "Why did you send me a snake?"

"The belt, you mean?" Chase shrugged, confused. "Why not?"

"You know how scared I used to be. Of snakes."

"I guess I forgot."

"Forgot—you!"

"I swear. I just meant it as a keepsake."

A keepsake, like the bear rug and the coyote skull. A souvenir from the wilderness.

Then it was Chase's turn. "What you said about life being wasted on me—"

"I shouldn't have said that, it isn't true. At least, no more for you than for anybody."

"Even if it is true, it's not the same as me wasting my life. You know?"

"I know." Roger flinched and squirmed, but he did not look away.

"I do want to be happy. I believe it still could happen."

Roger whispered, "It could."

"What about you?" Chase said.

"What do I want? Well." Embarrassed, Roger took a sip from his empty cup. "Happiness, of course. And I'd like to find somebody, before it's too late. And relax." He picked up the coffee pot, split the dregs between his cup and Chase's. "Last night when I was trying to sleep, I thought of the day we found the snake nest in the hedge. Do you remember?"

"I let one crawl all over me." Chase touched his throat.

Roger said, "I remember."

They sat looking at each other. They used to do this on the seesaw when they were very small: find the spot where they balanced and hang there, breathless, wide-eyed, unwilling to move.

Roger's phone gave its digital chirp.

"You can answer it," Chase said.

"I know who it is. My partner, Margaret. She wants us to come to dinner at her house. She's trying to be nice. I mean, she is nice."

"Really?" Chase squinted.

Roger watched his brother struggle with doubt, suspicion, and whatever bad memories might apply to this new situation. Then he watched him try to push it all aside.

"OK. Let's do it." Chase tried to smile. "Maybe it won't be bad."

My Favorite Lies

The best lie I ever told was for my mother.

I was nine. She was thirty-seven. We were sitting on a freshly painted bench in the city park, just across from the Eliza Hopewell memorial drinking fountain and its famous base of silver dollars. My mother handed me a bag of cotton candy, pushed my hair off my forehead, and asked, "Did Daddy say bad things about me before he left?"

I wasn't very sad when my father moved out; it had been hard to like him. But I couldn't make myself repeat the things he'd said so many times. I picked at the furry blue candy. I counted silver dollars. I sniffed the new paint in the air—it smelled nice. "He said you were a good secretary," I said, "but he told me not to tell." My mother smiled, and I was sure that I'd convinced her. Later I found out that my sister, two years older, had already told her the truth.

To this day my mother tells people that Sophie is her honest child and I am her kind child. And, she always quickly adds, "Every woman should have one of each."

Now Sophie perches on a blistered nightstand in the back of my refinishing shop, digging through her giant purse, which is round and gray and wrinkled like a brain. I'm crouched beneath her, scraping varnish off a sideboard.

"This time I'm really worried about Mom," she says, but since she says this at least once a month I don't stop scraping.

"Look what I found. Sitting on her television."

Sophie is holding up a framed photograph of Douglas MacArthur. The picture appears to have been pared down from an ancient magazine cover; the old soldier's face is cobwebbed with white paper creases.

"Valerie, does this look normal? Tell me the truth."

Sophie is a tall, open-faced person given to loud-slapping san-dals and impatient waves of the hand. A licensed therapist, she advises her patients to be scrupulously frank with themselves and their loved ones. Sometimes I actually shudder when I think of the misery my sister must cause.

"Normal doesn't equal happy," I say. I've always admired the way my mother uncomplainingly works her way through life. Like a swan, she never shows how hard she's paddling. But I must admit, this does look peculiar.

Sophie says, "If you think that Mom—Jesus, what's that sound?" Squeaking noises are creeping in the open door of my shop.

"Just the plant, an old gate or something."

"It makes my skin crawl." She shows me her goose-bumpy arm.

I rent a shed across the street from Hopewell Company Chemical Works #4. For the last year the plant has been chained up, silent but for the occasional protest of weary metal. Our mother worked there, in the manager's office, before she got laid off. Our father worked there too, before he transferred back to headquarters in Delaware.

"There's something else," Sophie says. "I went to see her yes-terday morning, when I knew she'd be home. She didn't answer the door, so I walked around back—"

"You know, Sophie, right now you sound like a very loving, concerned stalker."

"Listen. When I walked around back, I could see her standing on the deck, just looking out at the canal—"

"So?"

"So she was holding her wig, like this." Sophie mimes such a confused and poignant cuddle that I stop scraping and sit back on my heels.

"Let's take her out for lunch," Sophie says. "Her birthday's Saturday; it's the perfect excuse. Then we can find out what's going on. OK?"

"Fine." I manage not to roll my eyes.

On her way out, Sophie picks up my can of paint stripper and reads off the label. "'Inhalation of vapors may cause permanent brain and nervous system damage.' I'm amazed that Alan—a physician!—lets you endanger yourself this way."

"He doesn't see a problem." He nags me all the time.

I would never admit to Alan or my sister that sometimes even I worry about the way my lungs feel after I've stripped an especially stubborn piece of furniture. It's always worth it later, when I'm priming the piece for its new life. This sideboard, for instance, started out a morbid mahogany; in a week it will be staunch Shaker green, desirable once more.

I take the can away from Sophie, set it with the others, all tightly capped on a high shelf. "I know what I'm doing."

"So you've said." She cradles her heavy bag in her arms. "I'll call Mom and set up lunch."

"Then we'll get to the truth." As I say this, I can't help smiling at Sophie.

"Valerie, you wouldn't know the truth if it jumped up and killed you." But she can't help smiling at me.

She's right; I am a liar. For the usual reasons, to spare people's feelings and keep myself out of trouble. There's one thing I know: Lies hold people together. When my mother asks me if I plan to stay here in Hopewell, I say, Yes, where else would I go? When Sophie stretches out on my rag rug and tells me she's lonely, I tell her I'm lonely too, though this worked better before I started seeing Alan.

I met him six months ago. He was my gynecologist, just once, filling in for my usual doctor. He had rimless glasses and a long, inquisitive face, and he gave me his hand to shake before pulling up a stool and setting to work.

A stork mobile twirled above me. I said, "Aren't you going to tell me I'll just feel a little pinch?"

He said, "I don't know what you'll feel." I looked up in surprise, but all I could see were my own sheeted knees.

He said, "Does it hurt?"

I was about to lie and tell him yes, because I was embarrassed and because it almost did hurt. Then I thought, Be specific, there's hurt and there's hurt, hangnail and car crash, and by the time I'd formulated my qualified no, he was finished.

When he comes by tonight and asks about my day, I won't tell him that I inhaled evil fumes, picked on Sophie, and silently worried about my mother holding her wig. I won't tell him that after Sophie left I drove by my mother's apartment and when I saw that she was home I kept on driving. Why tell any of this when it's so much nicer to skip over it, go straight to wine, dinner for two, sex on the rag rug, and a long lazy conversation about the places we want to move to. He favors California; I'm partial to foreign lands. Tonight we'll scratch each other's feet and weigh our options. By then, today will be far behind me.

It's odd, but I've noticed that I can't seem to lie to Alan. Maybe when I know him better. I'm hoping.

Half an hour before the birthday luncheon, I'm parked, honking, outside our old house. Sophie lives here now, alone. My mother moved out ten years ago, to the apartment by the canal.

Sophie has made a few improvements. The shrubs now are squarely pruned, and the rooms get aired twice weekly, rain or shine. But I don't like coming here. For one thing, she's never changed the paint, a soiled gray, despite my professional recommendation of cream or vanilla. Also, she's set up her therapy office in our old room. Then there's the grandfather clock. Our father sent it to us five years ago. It arrived at the house in a long pine crate addressed to both of us. Sophie installed it beside her sofa, where it bongs mightily every fifteen minutes. Tempus Fugit, it says on its brass face, above an etching of a man with a clock head running for his life.

As Sophie doesn't have many therapy patients yet, she supports herself with another job, running the city recycling program. This involves nagging a community of ninety thousand and sometimes driving a truck. The paper just did an article on her, headlined, "Waste Not, Want Not: Chem-town's Leading Lady of Litter." No matter that the chemical company is gone for good, Hopewell's age-old nickname persists.

My sister bursts out of her front door, pursued by the bells of noon. Today she's all primary colors, circles and stripes, as forthright as a flag. As soon as she gets into my car, she spots an empty soda can and tucks it into her purse. "I was saving it for you," I say.

She grimaces, settling her gray purse between us. "I didn't sleep at all last night; I kept thinking about Mom's unemployment running out. She can't have many weeks left. Then what?"

"I guess she'll find another job."

"Doing what? She doesn't know computers. And it's not like we can help her much financially. Don't you ever worry about this?"

Constantly. But privately. I steer around an open manhole with a green hard-hat sticking out of it, then turn on to our mother's block. She's standing at the curb wearing a peach silk dress, new silver hair, and high, high heels.

"Girls." She arranges herself in the back seat, catching one shoe on the carpet. "Tell me I look great."

I say, "You do. Look great."

"Oh, a new wig," Sophie says.

My mother sighs. "Well, Sophie, if that's the best you can do." Her wigs are lustrous, lovingly tended, and almost undetectable. "I bought it last week; I thought it suited my new age. Fifty-eight sounds a lot older than fifty-seven, don't you think?"

"So stay fifty-seven," I say. "Who'll know?"

She starts to say something, cuts herself off. She's holding her neck stiffly, as if the wig weighs a lot. "It's not that easy," she finally says, as we pass Chemical Works #4. "Step on it, Valerie. It's my birthday, you know, and I'm starving."

Alan grew up in a matter-of-fact Catholic family where people yelled and blamed but never dreamed of leaving. He keeps asking me about my father, why I'm not in touch with him. "Was he violent? Drunk? Perverted?"

No. No. No. He was a manager at the company. He had a secretary, a suede desk blotter, a speaker phone, and a silver-paint-
ed model of a battleship that we weren't allowed to touch when
we visited his office. He had a crew cut and a set of barbells and
a backyard trampoline. I've told Alan all this many times over.

My mother is much easier to sum up for strangers:

Allentown, Pennsylvania. Dead father, hostile stepmother.
She left on her eighteenth birthday, armed with patent leather
pumps and a portable typewriter.

A secretary. Thirty-eight years of coffee grounds and paper cuts.

Divorced. First she said, "The company called Daddy back to
headquarters." Then, a few months later, when Sophie nagged
for details, "You won't hear me say a bad word about him." And
she never mentioned him again unless Sophie asked.

Boyfriends once, but no longer. The men in Hopewell are too
down in the mouth to fuss with.

Laid off.

Fifty-eight.

Two daughters, one honest, one kind.

Despite its name, the Lobster Trap restaurant sits not on an
ocean, or even on a lake, but on the Hopewell Canal, once an
artery of commerce, now a conduit for beer cans and unambi-
tious ducks. The canal smells like a wet old sneaker, but after all
these years we're used to it, so we don't mind eating on the
patio. Besides, it's a fluttery late September day, one of the last
warm ones we'll get. Sun simmers all around us, flashing off our
water glasses, broiling the part in my hair. Across the canal we
can see the frayed edge of downtown Hopewell.

My mother seems to be in a good mood, or at least is hiding a
bad one. "A see-through face is as cheap as a see-through
blouse"—that's what she always used to tell us. She orders a
martini, a lobster, and a small steak, then sits studying my hands,
stained Shaker green today. Her own coral-polished fingertips
are picking her cocktail napkin into shreds. When she sees me
looking, she puts her hands in her lap and says, "How's Alan?"

"Fine. Busy."

"That's nice." My mother likes Alan, but she's awkward around him. She can't put it out of her mind that he looks at women's private parts for a living.

A young man, thin and bare-chested, is struggling to push his kayak through the green, motionless water of the canal. My mother watches him anxiously. "What if he tips?"

"It's not very deep," Sophie says.

"But darling, it's so filthy, old chemicals and I don't know what else."

That's what we in Hopewell all wonder: What did the company leave behind? I mean, besides the obvious. What's seeping into us, blowing through us, as we try to mind our own business?

"So." I lift my wine glass, then realize I don't have a toast.

"To whatever comes next!" My mother gives an extravagant wink that seems to encompass me, Sophie, the canal, and the Hopewell skyline. "After lunch, let's go to the park."

Sophie says, "What for?"

"I haven't been there for so long. Remember, we used to go when you were little?"

"Dimly," I say.

"The zoo was fun, but it just shut down," Sophie points out.

"Yes," my mother says, "I do see the papers from time to time, believe it or not. If you don't mind my saying so, you girls are regular pills today."

Sophie glances at me, sits up straighter. "Mom, sometimes we worry about you."

"Sometimes I worry about the both of you, but you don't hear me harping on it, do you?"

I'm not offended, just surprised. "What do you worry about?"

"The usual things. But what's the point of harping? Uh-oh." The kayaker tips sideways, rights himself.

"He isn't making much progress," I say.

"I don't think he's trying to get anywhere, I just think he's enjoying the day." This time he flips all the way over in the jade-green water. "Poor thing."

Our lobsters arrive, scalded and fragrant. "They're getting smaller all the time," my mother says, twisting off a claw. "Remember those beauties your father used to buy?"

"Yes," Sophie says.

"No," I say.

"You were probably too young," my mother says. "Anyway, he's back."

Sophie and I sit identically frozen in place, plastic bibs on our chests, hot lobsters in our fists.

"Actually, he's been in town for a few weeks now, wrapping things up for the company. He's stopped by a few times. He looks healthy, still so trim and tan. He's grown out that awful crew cut."

Sophie says, "Why hasn't he called me?"

My mother scratches under the silver wig. "He did ask about you, and you too, Valerie."

"That's nice," I say.

"There's no need to be sarcastic," my mother says. "He's well aware of your attitude toward him. He says you never even thanked him for that clock he sent."

Sophie pushes her chair back, scrapes forward, pushes back again. "Mom, I have to tell you how I feel about this." My mother patiently tilts an ear at Sophie and sucks on a briny straw of lobster leg. "I don't think it's good for you to see him until you resolve some things. Maybe you should talk to someone."

"Darling, I am talking to someone." She flags the waitress for a second martini.

But for the next fifteen minutes we don't talk, we just pick at our lunches. There's a nerve-racking, nonstop squealing sound in the distance, like bad car brakes. Sophie can't seem to sit still. Her gray purse shifts on her lap like a fretful child. I feel like a baby too, ridiculous in my bib and hungry for a tantrum. It's not fair, him coming back!

My mother has always eaten quickly. Now, waiting for me and Sophie to finish, she arranges broken pieces of shell to form a nearly perfect lobster on her plate. Then she kicks each of us with a sharp-toed shoe. "Don't get all mopey on my birthday."

"I'm not moping," I tell her.

"Me neither," Sophie says. "I just feel—"

"I'm fine," my mother says. "Why wouldn't I be? I have my girls and my life and, I hope, some future. And, of course, all my memories." She laughs, pushing away her reconstituted lobster. "And I have my lovely canal."

"Mom," I say, "if you ever need money—"

"Valerie, I said I feel fine." She bites down on each word. "In fact, I feel great!" With this she raises her cup of melted butter, toasts us, and swallows.

Sophie closes her eyes. I lift my own cup of butter, though I refrain from drinking it. "That's great, Mom," is all I say.

"Should we go now?" Sophie says, in a quiet voice.

My car is parked by the canal, where a dropped sweater lies soaked on the bank and a lone duck paddles in circles. My mother stands watching the bird. She sniffs the warm September air. Suddenly, she groans, just a little. "Girls, why do we stay here?"

"We don't have to stay," I say, hopefully.

Sophie says, "I like it here. I do. The people and the hills and all the old houses. And things are starting to happen, like recycling."

My mother puts an arm around each of us. It's hard to tell if she's embracing or just leaning. "What about you, Valerie?"

"I've been happy here," I say, grudgingly.

"OK then," my mother says, squeezing us both, a little clumsy on her high shoes. "All right."

My parents always fought in silence, and they fought at the drop of a hat. A chance word or gesture, an insult impossible for anyone else to decode, and suddenly they were in combat, eyes burning, lips pressed tightly together against what might be said, willing the anger and tension into flame as Sophie and I watched in wonder.

They had their last fight when I was nine, on a humid July evening full of bugs. Maybe they were fighting about dinner. My mother had overcooked the steaks again so that we couldn't cut them; we had to gnaw them in our hands. Mosquitoes were whining and nipping at us. Sophie wasn't there; she must have been at her friend's house. My mother pushed her unfinished dinner away, then sat smoking and picking wax drips off the candles while my father stubbornly worried his meat. His pink scalp showed through his velveteen crew cut. I yawned over my ice cream and was glad when they sent me to bed.

I'd been asleep for a while when I heard rhythmic squeaking outside my window. My father was jumping on the trampoline, as he often did after an unpleasant dinner. I got up and leaned on the sill, watching him as he bounced up and down, still wearing his suit pants and white shirt.

When he saw me, he stopped. "You ought to be sleeping." He was breathing hard. His shirt was pulled out.

"I can't."

"Want to come out and spot me? So I don't fall off?"

"You never fall off," I said.

"Come keep me company, then." He helped me out the window and set me down barefoot on the scratchy grass. A sickle moon hung above us.

For half an hour I stood there in my seersucker pajamas, feeling mosquitoes prick my ankles, watching his bare feet push off, push off, push off. I stood, and I listened.

My mother was a fat-ass and a slob. She used to depend on her looks but her looks were going, just notice her upper arms, the way they flopped. And her cooking! A cavewoman could do better. She didn't do anything well, not a single thing, except for being a secretary, and why did she need to keep doing that when he made good money? Maybe she liked her boss too much; I probably wouldn't understand. And so on and so forth, bouncing higher and higher on the canvas. I was careful to keep my fingers away from the pinching coils. It was nothing I hadn't heard a dozen times before.

"I'm thinking of leaving for good, what do you think of that?" This was new. He came to a stop, knees flexed so he wouldn't tip over. "I'm thinking, what's keeping me here?"

"The plant?" On the trampoline he was at least nine feet tall.

"Nah, they'd love to have me back at headquarters."

"Mom always says she wants to move."

"Forget your mother for a second."

I could see the light on in her room. She'd be sitting on the vanity bench brushing out her hair. Warm, smoky, sleepy. There would be just enough extra room on the bench for me.

"If the company wants you, you should go," I said.

He looked at me for a long time. Then he picked me up and set me back inside my open window, carefully, like I had little baby bones. I pulled the screen down, but he stood there for a while before climbing back on the trampoline. I fell asleep to squeaky springs and wet breathing, and the next week he was gone. Sophie and I didn't see him again for five years.

"Goodbye/Good Luck, Chem-town!" That's what a silver banner says, stretched over the entrance to the zoo. At this moment the animals are on their way to Georgia. The surrounding park remains, for now; it's Saturday, but there's almost no one here.

"We'll probably get lost, it's been so long," I say. But the park is just as I left it, years and years ago. The carousel's horses still rear, wild-eyed. Stone buffalo still hunch at the end of the footbridge. Nothing seems to have changed for the better or the worse. Scaly diving boards jut over the pool; the statue of Cletus Hopewell points through the trees to the canal. We wander up and down the asphalt paths, softly bumping against each other, knocking purses and wrists, not saying much. We reach the end of the Petunia Promenade, and suddenly we're there again, at the Eliza Hopewell fountain. The bench has been repainted many times by now, but it's the same one, and the fountain's silver dollars are intact. Oblivious, Sophie bends over the spout and takes a lengthy drink.

My mother and I sit down; she squeezes my hand. "Remember?" She's whispering. "Remember what you told me here, that time?"

"*Mom.*" I move a little ways down the bench. She's never brought this up before.

"Of all the fibs you've told me, dear, that's still my favorite. It was so delicate and thoughtful, a regular work of art. I've never forgotten it." She pries off her high heels, wincing. "But now it's time to tell the truth."

"Why?"

"Because I'm too tired not to."

Sophie doesn't hear any of this, she's leaning on the fountain, looking into the distance, toward the pool.

I can't help it, the thought of the pool makes me smile. "OK," I say, speaking up for my sister's benefit. "I have a true story for you. About my brilliant lies." My mother nods encouragingly; Sophie sits down to listen.

I say, "Remember how he used to bring us here for swimming lessons, that summer he came back?"

"You girls were teenagers. He was doing that project for the company."

He'd wait for us at the entrance to the park each Saturday afternoon, wearing an Olympic-style Speedo swimsuit and a red sweatshirt with the pointy hood drawn tight around his face. "He wanted to teach us to dive better," I said. "That was the whole reason for seeing us, remember? But I always lied and told him I had my period."

"All summer? And he believed you?" My mother starts to laugh.

"Of course he didn't believe me, but what could he do?" His accusing and somewhat wounded glances had only added to the pleasure of my lie.

"So it was me that had to dive, " Sophie says. For an hour and a half each week, she would throw herself off the high board, trying to straighten the angle of her descent, while kids from school snickered and our father stood by the edge of the pool with his arms crossed and his hood up, critiquing.

My mother and I are laughing, but Sophie's twisting her purse strap and frowning.

"Poor Sophie." My mother strokes my sister's hair.

"I thought you would have resolved this by now, Sophie," I tease. She glares at me with real hurt. "I'm sorry." I am. But

there's more to the story. "One day when Sophie was in the lock-
er room changing, he asked me if I thought he should come back
for good. So, Mom, I told him you had a boyfriend." I'm gig-
gling now, fourteen once more. "I said your boyfriend's name
was Carl and he drove a forklift."

Her smile hangs in place, warily beating its wings. "A
forklift."

"I knew that a forklift would bother him more than a
boyfriend." Her smile has folded up, but my teenage bravado
won't be contained. "I have to say, to this day that's one of my
favorite lies."

Sophie says, "It's strange that Dad never figured out what a
liar you are, Valerie."

"He didn't know me very well."

"Or me," she says. "Or he would have said a better good-bye."
He'd left notes on our dressers, wrapped around fifty-dollar bills
and business cards with his new phone number inked in.

"He did love you both, for whatever that's worth," my mother
says. "I should say, he does love you."

Again we fall silent, listening to the far-off carousel. My mother lifts her wig a little, as if airing out her thoughts. Sophie
kneads her big purse. I pick old paint off my knuckles, thinking,
Alan's going to want to meet him, and he'll want to meet Alan.
What will they say to each other? And what will I say to him,
when the moment comes and we're once more left alone?

Sophie picks a discarded beer can from beneath the bench. She
shakes out the last drops, rolls it between her palms. She says,
"What's the use of getting older and working things out if you
can't get away from them, finally?" Then she puts her face down
on her purse and cries.

"Ditto," I say.

"Girls, whoever said you could get away?" My mother's hair
is listing slightly to the right. For the first time ever, she looks
like a woman in a wig. She waits until Sophie stops crying, then
slowly works her puffy feet back into her shoes. "Girls, I think
it's time." She rises up on the ridiculous heels, steadying herself
with a hand on each of us.

When we drop Sophie off at her house, we can hear the grand-father clock bonging, all the way to the street.

My mother invites me in for tea, then doesn't make any. Instead, she paces her mint-green carpeting, picking her nail polish, watching me. I see that MacArthur's picture has been replaced on the television top and wonder for the twentieth time how Sophie managed to sneak it out of the apartment.

I pick up the cheap metal frame. "Where did this come from?"

My mother stands close, looking over my shoulder at the stubborn face. "He was trying to make a joke. You know, 'I shall return' and all that." She shakes her head. "Poor thing."

I say, "Is he going to stay?"

"Valerie, you know perfectly well that there's nothing left in Hopewell for a businessman." Suddenly, her voice is rising, hot. She pulls off the wig and tosses it onto the coffee table. Her own hair, speckled gray, is flattened to her skull with the stretched foot of an old stocking. She tears that off too and walks across the room to fuss with the cord of the window blinds.

I put the picture down, facing the wall. "Once he leaves, things can get back to normal."

"Normal?"

"You can have your own life again."

"You don't know what it's like." Her eyes are much larger without the wig. They look right at me.

"Well," I say.

"You don't know what my life is like." Half accusing, half pleading. How terrible when your mother looks at you this way, as if you can help her! She says, "I'm so tired. But you don't want to know."

"Sophie wants to know, and you won't tell her."

"I can't tell her these things, she takes them too much to heart."

"She has a see-through heart," I murmur.

"But you sure don't; you never did." My mother sighs, disgust-ed, snapping the blinds open and shut as if signaling for a rescue. "I don't understand you, Valerie. What did he do that was so bad?"

I pick paint from under my left thumbnail. She's waiting. "He said terrible things about you, all the time."

"Oh, come on." For the second time today, my mother groans.

"He did. Like he thought I was on his side. Or that if I stopped liking you, I might start liking him."

"Were they true?"

"What difference does that make?" Now I'm the one pacing. I push open the door to the deck and walk into the hot-sneaker smell of the canal. I'm thinking, We're fighting out loud.

"It matters," she said.

"The things he said were true, OK? But I told him something true too. I told him he should leave."

"And now you don't want to face him," she says.

Across the canal there's another apartment house just like this one. If I lean out over the deck railing, I can see my reflection in the water.

Again she stands close behind me. She says, "I know what he said about me. Sophie told, remember?"

"I don't know what he said to Sophie. She always tried to tell me, and I'd always run away." The water doesn't ripple or flow; my reflection just sits there. "Alan wants to go to San Francisco."

"I guess that's one solution," she says. "Poor Sophie. Dear God, I don't believe it. Look."

That same kayaker is headed toward us, sunburned now, and glazed with sweat. My mother calls to him. "Young man, are you thirsty? Would you like a soda?" He shouts back that he's fine, holds up a can of something. Once more we watch him fight his way past us.

All of a sudden I can't stand the sight of him. "What's he been doing down there all day?"

"Valerie, I'm sure it's none of your business."

She's right, of course.

Her real hair is so thin. I stifle my urge to reach over and fluff it up. Instead, I say, "What do the two of you talk about, these days?"

She pushes my bangs off my forehead. "What do you think? The only thing that's left. Our girls."

∞

I gave Alan a key to my house three weeks ago, but this is the first time he's let himself inside. There's an open bottle of wine, a pot of violets on the fireplace. He's reading a study of Victorian childbirth procedures, lying on his back on my rag rug, although the house is full of chairs I've refinished. I sit down beside him. From this angle on the floor I can see that a chair I did last year still isn't right; the white paint makes it look unfinished, merely primed. Maybe I should try dark blue or green, or even go back to the wood itself. "Maybe I'm stuck here for a while," I say.

For a long time he just looks at me. Then he looks at his socks. Finally, eyes fixed upon the argyle, he says, "I like it here."

"That's the worst lie I've ever heard." He doesn't understand that I'm making an artistic, not a moral, criticism. He can't figure out why I'm kissing him. "It's my favorite lie."

"Really, I do like Hopewell, the people and hills and all," he says.

"And the recycling."

"What?"

"Never mind."

By turning a little we can look out the window, down at Hopewell, at the scarred and browning hills, the churches, the familiar heap of chutes and smokestacks and storage tanks. The canal cuts its green path, east to west. And somewhere down there my mother sits waiting for the phone to ring.

"My back aches," I say. "We walked too far."

He lays me down on the rug, spreading me out like a wet sweater. He presses his hands into my spine, leaning into me, lending me his weight. My breath is squeezed out; I can't say much, so I contemplate the rug itself, the lint and dust, the unbreakable braids of some far-off woman twisting out her confusion.

He says, "So, was it good, your mother's big day?"

I fight for a breath. "Everybody got upset about something, but I guess everybody made up. Sophie cried." I keep my eyes on the rug. "My father's back."

"I know, he just called and left a message. He says he's staying at the Hopewell Ramada, and he really wants to talk to you, and don't forget that time flies. He sounded interesting; I hope I get to meet him."

Alan's fingers probe, hunting. The floorboards creak beneath us. I groan. He says, "Does it hurt?"

"A little," I tell him. "Maybe a lot."

The Nemesis

Every asshole believes he's a realist.

"I'm only stating the obvious, which for obvious reasons sounds trite: In this world, dogs eat dogs."

After each Wednesday meeting of the middle management productivity enhancement team, Ellis Mahar would lean back on his chair casters and clasp nine red fingers behind his neck, striving (I knew) for a posture both superior and devil-may-care. He would stretch out in the emptying conference room, claiming its light and length for himself, and as he did, we couldn't help staring at the soaked armpits of his monogrammed, too-tight shirts. They cast a high-pitched citrus scent.

"In love and war, it's kill or be killed. Take it from a purple-hearted veteran."

Dogs didn't eat dogs, of course, not even in the white slums of Charleston, which Ellis claimed as his birthplace. He had never fought in a war. But no one ever contradicted him; he was an asshole, and not worth the trouble.

I was the only person in the office who even acted like his friend.

"I think I'm in love," he said. "I'm going to have to nip it in the bud."

We were sitting on a bench in the new riverfront park, holding windblown lunches on our laps, watching strangers jog down the fresh asphalt paths. Transplanted cherry trees were blooming all around us; it appeared to be a fine day for love.

"Who is she?"

Ellis pulled a shard of onion from his sandwich and tossed it to a pigeon. "You don't know her." The pigeon dropped the onion and waddled away.

39

"Do you really mean 'in love'?"

"As opposed to common boning? I'm afraid so." His high pink brow pleated. "But it's out of the question."

I turned to face him. "Why?"

He paused, relishing my curiosity. His ears were so shiny that they appeared laminated. He must have spent a lot of time cleaning them. "Obviously, you've never been in love, Desda."

"Not irreversibly." Never. Was it that obvious?

Now it was his turn to stare at me.

"If I let this go on," he said, "I'll be putting myself at another person's mercy. Laying my neck on the block and saying, 'OK, sweetheart, start chopping.' Tell me why I need that in my life."

I knew he wanted me to beg him to fall in love, but I couldn't. It was bad enough to think about Ellis having sex. The idea of those heavy arms reaching out in honest heartsore need was more than I could stand.

"We should get back," I said. "I've got a one-thirty meeting."

"Desda?"

"Yes." I adjusted my headband, which despite its soft velvet cover clamped my temples just a little too hard.

"Don't tell anybody. OK?"

As if I would. My position as Ellis's lunchmate and confidante inspired enough jokes at the office. Our coworkers would be clustered in a cubicle or restaurant booth, painstakingly criticizing Ellis's opinions, manners, and monograms, when someone would notice me and break off, grinning. "Sorry Desda, I forgot, he's your friend." My denials only made them laugh harder.

In high school, I was the girl who dated the tuba player, the mouth-breather, the passionate hoarder of beetles and quartz—once each, and only because my mother hadn't been home to intercept their phone calls and say, "I'm sorry, Desda isn't here" (then come up to my bedroom and beg, "Please don't make me lie again." She'd been a genuinely compassionate person). If only I'd had plans, boyfriends, something to protect me. But no one else called, and when one of these deficient boys managed to corner me, I couldn't find the words to turn him down. Pity isn't compassion, though; it will only stretch so far. I'd go to the movie or tournament or lecture and sit beside my date so stiff and silent, so insulted by his very presence, that he wouldn't ask me out again. At college, with no mother to shield me, things got even worse.

What defenses did I have against Ellis Mahar?

No one else had any pity for him. Wasn't he a sexist, a racist, a troglodyte, a lout? Consider his remarks about welfare cases and immigrants; the homeless, mad, and addicted; all those who should be ground beneath the heels of society's triumphant middle managers. Worst of all, he was a bore. He liked to talk about Charleston, where none of us had been. His stories were highly detailed and slow to unfurl, and he'd lean close to tell them, as if proximity could ignite interest in the Mahars' ancestral teamsters and wharf rats, and his own brief season as a longshoreman. The last had cost him his right middle finger, something to do with a winch and a load of rice.

His personal philosophy was your basic undergraduate bastardization of Ayn Rand and Thomas Hobbes—selfishness, brutality, victory, and so forth—and he belabored it as relentlessly as Charleston. He did seem to read a lot. He'd speed-read the Upanishads and found them very shallow. Ditto the New Testament, that salt-lick for losers.

Maybe it was. I'd never read it. Ellis devoted a lot of energy to disproving the existence of God. No one else I knew even bothered.

He always delivered his credo with his eyebrows gathered and his voice lowered one circumspect notch, as if he were saying something that could get him imprisoned, something the rest of us had never considered. But who didn't accept that self-defense was the spine of our lives? We were in business, after all. We just knew better than to say it out loud.

Really, Ellis's greatest crime was his crudeness.

People were inventive at avoiding him. Once, planning a cross-country skiing party, my boss Judith said, "I suppose I should invite your friend Ellis." Without thinking, I said, "He won't go skiing; he's afraid to fall down. But he's not my friend." So she asked him to come, and he declined. Now people invited him skiing even when they weren't really going, knowing he wouldn't accept.

How did I know he was afraid to fall in front of us? I just did, the same way I could picture his narrow apartment windows and his wide, hard bachelor bed.

Ellis claimed to get laid fairly often, always by beauties with money and taste. But I knew he hadn't had many real girl-friends. ("Women push. You know what I mean. Don't you?") I doubted that he was really in love. I figured he was trying to make some point about life in the jungle. Still, I thought I could imagine the woman he might, if not love, at least fall for: good teeth, taut body, bright blue dress. Decent diction, blond streaks. A degree in public relations from one of our nation's finest foot-ball schools. Ellis never understood what gave him away.

"You don't know her," he'd said. So it couldn't be someone at work.

In any case, I knew it wasn't me. My relationship with Ellis was based upon a frank, mutual lack of attraction. We'd dis-cussed it. He was a boaster and a barbarian, I was a virgin and an oddball, and that, we'd agreed, was that.

The next time Ellis and I returned, lunch bags in hand, to the bench beside the cherry trees, we found that we couldn't sit still. Spring was bumptiously pushing forward. Pink blossoms were dropping, branches were fizzing up green, and the air swirled fragrant with mud and pollen, dragging people out of their offices and into the park. Some marched, some ran, some stum-bled as if they were dreaming. Ellis and I tried to eat as we walked.

A fat woman hurried past us. Ellis pointed a celery stick at her rear and tried to say something insulting, but his mouth was too full to speak.

"Are you on a diet?" I asked.

He nodded and gulped. "Now you, Desda, you're beyond vanity."

"I am?"

"Don't take that the wrong way. I just mean that you don't have to give it a thought. Because you're rich."

I no longer bothered to point out that I wasn't rich. I knew what he meant. My trust fund barely would have paid the rent on my apartment, but the mere fact that I had one was enough to impress Ellis.

He said, "You look fourteen and dress like sixty. Life bounces off you like mercury. But it doesn't matter, and you know why? Because you have money."

Maybe, but the manic breeze was tousling my hair and pushing my skirt above my knees. Usually, I had trouble keeping up with Ellis's much-longer legs, but that day he seemed to be dragging his feet, while I was impatient to move faster. It was hard to eat and walk at the same time, and I was weeping from the pollen; I threw my sandwich in the trash.

Ellis said, "I'm not faring too well with this love-killing thing."

"Leave it alone. It'll die on its own."

"How do you know?"

"I read."

My words surprised me no less than Ellis, who laughed so frankly that he sounded like someone else entirely, and fastened his round blue eyes on me.

"Desda, how old are you?"

"Twenty-nine."

"That used to be old, for a woman."

"You're thirty-five."

"It's different for me."

"How is it different? Because you're a man?"

"You know why. Because I'm an asshole." He played with his necktie and tried to laugh. "You have to help me."

A young man in shorts flew past us, all tendons and calves, kicking up his heels as he ran, and at that moment I wanted a crush. Not love, just something to justify the weather. Despite what I'd implied to Ellis, I did get crushes from time to time, always with inappropriate objects. Once on the technical support man who blew dust out of my keyboard. Once, I'm sorry to

say, on my boss Judith's handsome, elderly husband.
Fortunately, these infatuations always knuckled under to common sense and the demands of the day.

Ellis said, "Are you OK?"

The runner's bare legs disappeared around a curve. I dabbed
my eyes. "It's this weather."

Ellis tossed his lunch bag toward a trash can; it missed. He
tried to walk away, but I pinched him through his tight sleeve. I
think this was the first time I touched him. "Don't be an asshole," I said.

When he bent down to pick up the bag, I could hear his knees
pop.

He sighed. "I'm gonna get murdered."

Selfishness, not pity, inspired me to invite Ellis to my father's
house for the weekend. I didn't want to go there alone, and I
trusted that even if Ellis noticed things, he wouldn't know how
to add them up. Anyway, there was no one else to ask.

I'd gone back three times in two years and on each visit found
the house and its master in greater disorder. How I missed my
mother! She'd always managed to treat my father kindly, and
although he only laughed at her when she was alive, he fell into
disrepair once she was gone. When he'd had enough to drink,
he would almost admit it. Untended, his natural meanness and
self-loathing had sent out shoots in every direction, and I was
powerless to prune them back. I carefully measured out forty-
two hours per visit and spent most of that time reading old
books in my old room.

As much as he could cherish anything, my father cherished
his mahogany Herreshoff. Though of modest size, the sailboat
was quite old, and impressive to connoisseurs; when Ellis and I
arrived, I could see it rearing and bucking at the dock, as if
delighted to see us.

The Nemesis. That's what my father had insisted on naming it.

He claimed to enjoy sailing, but what he really enjoyed was
humiliating pretenders to the nautical lifestyle. Ellis knew just

enough to get himself in trouble. Before we'd finished our first drinks, my father had drawn him out on the subject of sailing and gently set the noose about his throat.

"God, I love the water! Given my druthers, Mr. Stone (may I call you Ted?), I'd pack in the job for six months and set off for Aruba."

My father pushed a strand of graying hair behind his ear and, with malicious generosity, offered to let Ellis take the boat out on the water.

"Oh—" Ellis shook his ice cubes.

"I insist. God knows Desda has no interest in sailing."

"Maybe if there's time on Sunday—"

"Fine. But remember, I won't take no for an answer."

Sitting beside Ellis, I could smell his underarms heating up, casting their familiar scent of oranges and disinfectant.

I knew that my father would spend the entire weekend threatening to make Ellis go sailing, for the sheer pleasure of seeing the high pink face tighten and flinch, and hearing the soft Charleston tongue change the subject. So I filled the next day with a tour. We drove up and down the coast, out to the light-house, then back to town. We walked around the green, past the churches and daffodils and my grandfather's memorial flag-pole. At one point I asked Ellis how his love affair was pro-gressing, but to my surprise he refused to discuss it.

He stopped short on Main Street, tilting a shiny ear.

"It's so quiet here. Listen." Gulls. A passing Jeep. A hammer on the library roof. "Everything's been settled, hasn't it? The spoils have been divided. They've chased the losers away. Now there's nothing left but the victors, all tucked in to die."

He did not make this assertion with his usual glee. Indeed, his forehead gathered as we watched ancient Lila Pratt teeter down the sidewalk, pressing a five-and-dime bag to her chest. Every day she walked two miles into town, bought a pack of playing cards, then crept back home. She appeared to be sporting the same threadbare Keds she'd worn throughout my childhood.

Ellis whispered, "I bet she's richer than God."

"She is."

"I bet she's the last person she knows."

That night I let Ellis help me make dinner. I couldn't leave him to my father, who was lying in wait on the deck, armed with a tall glass and a copy of *Wooden Boat* magazine. As I'd hoped, Ellis didn't say anything about the kitchen; he pretended not to notice the burned-out lightbulbs, rusted carving knives, and mouse droppings. Maybe he'd seen as bad in gothic Charleston.

When we went in to dinner, I steered Ellis away from my mother's chair, to a seat on my father's left, where I hoped he would be sheltered from scrutiny.

My mother used to say she fell in love with my father because of the delicacy and consistency of his table manners. No matter how much he'd had to drink, he could peel a piece of fruit with panache. Now his elbow ground the tablecloth as he propped his head upon his hand. Salt and crumbs speckled his sleeve. This did not prevent him from keeping a close eye on Ellis's fork and knife.

I watched Ellis cramp under the inspection, stiffly moving his fingers, his big arms pressed tight to his sides. The conversation staggered and keeled over. Before long, all three of us were staring forlornly at my mother's chair.

"Ellis," I said, "why don't you tell a Charleston story?"

He set down his fork and embarked on a long tale about a spinster, a pirate, and a hidden passageway.

"That's a good one," I said, and I meant it.

"It happens to be true," he said, pleased.

My father blotted his lips on his wrist. "You Southerners surely have the gift of gab."

Ellis put his hands in his lap.

"The South is a more verbal culture," I pointed out.

"Yes, daughter, I've read that." He turned to Ellis. "But I happen to be from Rhode Island."

"Ah."

"I don't suppose that means much."

Ellis blinked, nodded, shrugged, then turned to me with desperation.

"Let's clean up the kitchen," I told him. "At least, let's try."

On the last afternoon I stood with my father on the deck, watching Ellis walk up from the beach. His chinos were too tight, and his long arms were swinging.

My father stirred his drink with his middle finger. "Your friend strikes me as very . . ." I waited for the subtly insulting adjective: outgoing (vulgar), ambitious (grasping), intelligent (crafty). "Hearty and hale," he finally said.

I knew what he wanted me to say: "He's not my friend!" But I denied him the satisfaction. "Ellis used to be a longshoreman," I said. "That's how he hurt his hand."

And we had nothing more to say until Ellis joined us. He accepted a glass of my father's nastiest whiskey and stood between us, sipping with barely a flinch, watching *The Nemesis* nudge the dock.

My father checked his watch. "Well, Desda, your obligation is just about fulfilled. I suppose you're already packed."

"Yes. We should get going."

Through our pressed sleeves, I felt Ellis sag with relief. He took a long sip of his drink and looked around. "You have a beautiful home, Mr. Stone."

"It's my mother's," I said.

The roads back to the city were snarled and bitter with exhaust. Ellis and I barely spoke or looked at each other. I couldn't tell if I was sorrier for myself or for him, and I suspected he felt the same way. When I dropped him off, he took my hand, squeezed it and carefully replaced it on the steering wheel. It was only after I'd parked under my own building that the thought occurred to me.

What if Ellis really was in love, with a woman who really existed? What if this woman was me?

It wasn't completely out of the question. He liked to spend time with me, maybe by default, but he did. He claimed to find me interesting, as few men had. He confided in me. I cringed, now, to think of all the times I'd let him go on about the women he'd allegedly boned and banged and bagged. He'd probably thought I was interested, when in fact I'd only been acting polite. There might have been a little curiosity, but nothing more than that.

Shyness and shame, those were concepts I could manage. Even lust, to a point. If Ellis merely wanted to bone me, that was one thing. But he'd spoken of love, which had never crossed my mind, not toward myself. Is that hard to believe? Pathetic? Maybe, but the fact was, I couldn't begin to imagine it.

I pulled off my headband; I pressed my aching temples like my mother used to do. I decided to call Judith. She was the woman I wanted to be: cool-brained, smooth-browed, unblushing. "Ellis Mahar loves me." That's what I would say—no, "Ellis Mahar might love me," and she would tell me what to do. First I practiced saying the words out loud, because I didn't want to laugh. Then I breathed deeply and dialed Judith's number. When her handsome, elderly husband answered, I burst out crying and hung up, praying he wouldn't care enough to check back and find out who I was. He didn't.

"Nip it in the bud." That was the expression Ellis had used, that first day in the park, and that was what I set out to do. I turned down his lunch invitations, avoided him after the Wednesday productivity meetings and carefully did not look to see how he was reacting.

A freak snowstorm blew through at the end of April, scalding flower buds and chasing people out of the park. Judith suggested that we all take another skiing trip to make the best of the situation, and I eagerly agreed, craving winter's simplicity and order. But almost no one wanted to ski. Only the new woman in my department and Lance from human resources, whose face I could never quite remember. And Ellis.

"It's high time I learned cross-country," he said.

Judith borrowed her husband's Jeep for the trip. She invited the new woman, Joleen, to sit up front with her. There was lots of luggage, which left little room in the back seat for me, Ellis, and Lance. As we climbed the mountain, lurching over frost heaves and switchbacks, my knees bounced back and forth between the men; my arms were cramped from holding tightly to myself. Ellis sat behind Joleen, dividing his attention between her blond-streaked head and the passing view.

At twilight the landscape turned mean. All color drained away. Tree boughs sagged under their weight of snow, and boulders blackly loomed on every side. Ellis all but pressed his nose to the Jeep's smoked-glass window. "This is brutal, isn't it? If you got lost here, you'd never get back alive."

"Yes, you would," I said. "With all the condo people and bigfoot tourists, someone would be bound to stumble over you. The problem up here is getting away from everyone."

Joleen turned around, inspecting me with large, amused eyes. "Desda, are you PMS-ing?"

Lance tried not to laugh, and I realized that they thought I was an asshole. Ellis, meanwhile, had gone back to staring out the window.

By the time we got to the lodge, I ached all over from clutching myself for five hours. I despised Joleen and Lance with the savor that only bruised pride can provide. But at least I'd come to doubt my theory that Ellis might love me. Like other of my private epiphanies, it simply didn't hold up in the glare of real life.

The next morning, Ellis insisted on going off to ski by himself.

"You were right," Judith told me as we laced up our boots. "He doesn't want to fall down where we can see him. Doesn't he know that's a good way to get in with people?"

"He thinks he'd get eaten alive."

"By us? I suppose we might nibble a little, just around the edges." She smiled at me and yanked her laces tight. "But that's life, isn't it? Give and take, and sometimes you have to give."

"When you're on the bottom."

"He's not on the bottom, exactly. More like the lower-middle." Suddenly, I realized that Judith wasn't talking about social background but about the office, where Ellis and I were at the exact same level. She saw my expression; deftly, she redirected the conversation. "I'm surprised Ellis hasn't noticed that big, talky men don't do well at our company. You know? The guys who play their cards close, they're the ones who climb."

That whole day my skis felt out of control. I kept stabbing with my poles, growing more and more self-conscious, which made me even more clumsy and desperate to stab. I skied in the middle of the group, in front of Lance, behind Joleen's pale, swinging ponytail. As I struggled down the trails, I tried to imagine the sort of mother who would name a child Joleen. I didn't like to be a snob, but still, one had to wonder.

By the end of the day, I'd concluded that Lance and Joleen were definitely lower than Ellis and me, but probably not enough to matter much to Judith.

Ellis met us at the lodge for drinks and dinner, and for once he didn't hold forth on Charleston, Darwin, or anything else. He sat quietly, wincing a little when he moved, and I was amazed to see Judith compete with Joleen to draw him out. She was a little drunk. When she leaned close to him and said, "Ellis, you are not nearly on the bottom," I excused myself.

Back in my room I fell prey to an all-out allergy attack. I wept, I gasped, I shrieked with sneezes. I called the front desk and insisted that they move me to one of the nonallergenic rooms advertised in small print on the back of the lodge brochure. Half an hour later, dosed with antihistamines, propped up on steril-ized pillows, I started to sleep.

That's when the hissing started, just outside my window. A faint, whispery sound, laced with something like a human moan. They'd moved me to the ground floor, in the back of the building. I got up to investigate, still weeping a little, but I could see only black woods and a blue slope of moonlit snow. I was just about to go back to bed when a skier flew past me. It was Ellis. I cranked open my window and watched him. His cross-country skis were too long and clumsy for the steep hill, but he managed to stay upright until he reached the bottom, where he rammed full-speed into a plowed snowbank. The bank was high and rough-looking, studded with chunks of road asphalt. Ellis embed-ded himself so deeply that it took him a long time to dig free.

He struggled to take off the skis and dragged them behind him as he trudged up the hill. At the top, he stepped back into the bindings, then plunged down once more, straight into the snowbank.

He didn't know how else to stop himself.

I watched him go up and down the hill for half an hour. Every time he passed my window—knees locked, impotently waving his poles—he groaned the same two words: "Dear God."

It wasn't that he was afraid to fall in front of us. He was afraid to fall at all.

I debated whether to reveal myself. I could tell him how to stop—even climb out the window and demonstrate in my nightgown. But that would mean admitting I'd seen him crash and heard him pray, and that would ruin his night. He'd think I was gloating, inwardly feasting on his weakness.

But wasn't that what he claimed to expect? Wasn't that his point when he fixed his eyes upon us and quoted Thomas Hobbes—that life was hard, a battlefield, an abattoir, and people irreversibly cruel? Or did he want us to argue with him?

There had always been an odd insistence to Ellis's social analyses, as if each day he was freshly surprised by the harshness of the world. Maybe he hadn't meant it when he said, "In this world, dogs eat dogs." Maybe he really wanted what he'd demanded that day in the park: "Tell me why I need love in my life."

The next morning, both of us were bruised and sore. Judith invited me to sit up front for the ride back to the city. I didn't speak to Ellis until midnight, when I pushed aside a lifetime of good judgment and knocked at his apartment door.

He lived halfway up a forty-floor building, one of the new high-rises built along the river. The security man at the front desk glanced at me and waved me on. This always happened, and I'd always thought it was because I looked so respectable, but in Ellis's lobby mirror I saw what the security man must have seen: a ninety-pound woman with knock-knees and pollen-chafed eyes. No threat to anyone, barely worth noticing.

Ellis answered his door in a silk robe that might have made a smaller man look elegantly relaxed; it made him look like a weary prizefighter. He was so surprised to see me that he didn't ask me in. I had to stand in the dimly lighted hall to say what I'd come to say:

"My father never takes the boat out. He doesn't sail. I don't think he really knows how."

Ellis didn't respond, just pulled on the armpit of his robe. His silence made me say something I hadn't planned.

"The wonderful thing about my mother was, she never said a word. He'd go on about jibs and booms and coming about, and she would just smile and nod like he knew what he was saying."

"But she was a rich girl, isn't that what you said?"

"She came from a little money."

"And I bet he was a poor boy."

"He's not from the Rhode Island he implies."

"So she could afford to be generous."

"No, that wasn't it at all." I turned to leave. For the first time since I'd met him, Ellis had managed to offend me.

"Sorry. Really. I'm being a . . . you know. Don't go." He stepped back and held the door open, looking down at his big bare feet.

He lived in a studio apartment with a plate-glass wall that offered a huge view of the southern suburbs. I sat on the sofa, trying to look out, but it was hard to see past my own reflection.

I said, "It wasn't just philanthropy on my mother's part."

"What was it?" He handed me a bottle of beer and sat down beside me, careful to keep his robe closed. There were bruises up and down his shins.

"It's a gift. It was, I should say. It was a gift for loving some-body. Not from charity, though, or from pity or even compas-sion."

"How, then?"

"I can't say. I don't have it."

He nudged me. "Come on. Spit it up."

My knees ground against each other. My heart thumped as it ventured down the slippery trail. "Because somehow, against all the evidence to the contrary, you see something to love. And somehow it's enough."

He clicked his bottle against mine, and we sat back, watching our reflections in the big window: Ellis with his too-tight armpits and his proud-and-frightened face; me, clutching my own shoulders, my headband askew from the late hour and the oddness of it all.

"My arms hurt," I said. "I skied wrong."

"I can't ski at all. But so what?" He leaned back and crossed his ankles, clasping nine fingers behind his neck. "Winter's all done, at least for now."

Myra

My next door neighbor wants to name her baby Myra. I think she is making a big mistake. I would like to hear from other Myras to see if they dislike their name as much as I do.

Myra Ritter
111 Union Avenue
641-7313

Myra waited three weeks for the newspaper to print her letter, but when it finally appeared she couldn't read it; she could only push the page away and walk in nervous circles around her kitchen. She felt brave and foolish, too big and too small. It was a rainy May morning that smelled of new grass and earthworms, the sort of day she used to like to walk in, but now she didn't want to leave her telephone.

The calls began at noon.

"Hello, is this Myra?" The voice was thin and tight but eager to please. "My name is Myra Box-Smith, and I love my name. You should love yours too."

"Tell me why," Myra said, sitting on the edge of her late husband's recliner.

"For one thing, our name is Latin for Wonderful One! Myra, I can help you."

Myra invited Mrs. Box-Smith to lunch the next day, then jumped up smiling and read her printed letter six times in a row.

She got a few other calls that afternoon, one from an angry man whose beloved late wife was named Myra, one from a Myrna who needed help making bail, and one from a numerologist who offered her a discounted consultation. She took all the calls politely, making notes with a sharp pencil, marveling at how easy it was to reach other people. She was disappointed not to hear from more Myras, but at sundown the phone rang once more.

"I'm Myra Hyde, and you're right about the name, but I'm eighty-three and it's too late to do anything about it." This voice was sticky and strong, like hot tar.

"I'm seventy," Myra said.

"I begged my mother to let me change my name to Dolores, but she wouldn't. Her name was Myra too."

Myra invited Miss Hyde to join her and Mrs. Box-Smith for lunch.

"I can't eat anything but my own food," Miss Hyde said.

Myra agreed to visit her the next week at her apartment, then hung up, feeling a little uncomfortable, as if the old lady's griping voice had stuck itself in her ear canal. She decided to take a bath and was just walking to the bathroom when the doorbell rang.

Her pregnant neighbor's bald husband, Ham, stood two steps down, holding a bunch of white lilacs. "Mrs. Ritter, I know you probably didn't mean anything by that letter, but Lisa cried all morning."

Myra sighed, looking down upon his forthright face. The Tozers were a pale, plump young couple with two jack-in-the-box children and a yard full of toys and dandelions. Sometimes they said grace before dinner; she could see them through her porch window.

Myra said, "I was just trying to warn her."

Ham peered around her at the silent living room. "Is everything OK?"

The Tozers always checked on Myra during snowstorms and offered her rides to the store, and although she appreciated this, she now found herself getting impatient. She said, "Tell Lisa I'm sorry, but I stand by my letter. I am appalled that the two of you would give my ugly name to an innocent child."

Ham stammered. "It sounds nice and old-fashioned, that's all. And we like you. Here." He handed her the lilacs.

She thanked him but held the flowers at arm's length. The Tozers' lilac bush grew halfway between their bedroom and Myra's. The high, sweet fragrance wasn't bad from a distance, mixed in with the smell of breakfast toast or Clorox, but when it pushed untamed into Myra's bedroom, it made her want to hide among the stale coats in the closet. Now, looking down at Ham, Myra suspected that despite what he'd just said, he was kind to her not because he liked her but merely because he was kind. Some people were nice because they were too stupid to be anything else.

This brand-new thought was swift and startling, like a cramp. It frightened her: She was not turning into the old woman she'd expected to be.

Ham said, "Why don't you like your name?"

"It's old, that's all." She glanced over her shoulder at the living room, the long-broken hi-fi, her husband's sagging tweed chair. The carpeting, once thick and gold, was stamped down like a pasture, with visible trails to the kitchen and bathroom. "It's all worn out."

Once she thought she'd be like the old women she used to know, women with parakeets, grandchildren, and flowered dresses soft from years of washing. She thought she would bake and fuss and pray; she would fall asleep prepared to wake in heaven. But by Myra's seventieth birthday, sugar hurt her teeth, God was as remote as ever, and her son was too busy making music videos in Europe to make her any grandchildren. She still liked thunderstorms and oysters and the smell of sweat on an honest man. She was the same self she'd always been. She was beginning to think that she'd never be ready to die, and this scared her as much as the suspicion that she had not turned into a good person.

She had taken up walking ten months before, after Monroe died, starting slowly and shyly but gradually forging a two-mile route across her corner of the city. She liked being outside on winter mornings, feeling her shoes crunch on the frosted sidewalks. Mainly, she liked looking in the windows of other houses. Myra was astonished by what people chose to show the world.

The hardest part of the walk was a three-block climb up a hill of old attached houses. Myra's chest and thighs would ache as she forced her way upward, but there was a reward at the top: an ornate, butter-colored Victorian whose curtains were always open, showing a plump red sofa and an ever-changing floral arrangement. One day Myra saw a couple sitting on the sofa, close together, passionately talking or maybe even arguing. She saw the woman catch the man's wrist and press it against her throat. Myra walked by the house every day for a month after that, but she never saw the people again.

In March she'd caught a chest cold that kept her indoors for three weeks. When she went walking again, she was out of shape and had to concentrate on each step. The hill was especially hard that first day. Her lungs felt roasted. She was almost past the house with the red sofa before she noticed that its facade had been draped with burlap. The cloth snapped in the wind, sooty and torn; when it lifted, Myra saw that the house had been stripped of paint. Only the dry, peeled shell remained, and the rooms inside were empty.

She stood on the windy sidewalk and shivered, breathing hot and hard, watching the rag of burlap rise and fall. Slowly, she made her way home, wondering what frightened her more, the empty house or the dirty cloth that covered it.

Myra tried walking a few more times after that, without much success. She couldn't get her wind back. The spring thaw made her bones hurt. She began to accept the Tozers' rides to the supermarket. Most of the time she stayed in, keeping her curtains pulled shut. She tried to rearrange the living room, but she wasn't strong enough. She tried to straighten out the paperwork Monroe had left behind, but for some reason she had to stop, disheartened, whenever she saw her own name.

The morning of the luncheon with Myra Box-Smith, Myra arranged a spring-fruit platter and prepared the ingredients for a cheese soufflé. She put on her pearls and her engagement ring and, for lack of other flowers, set the Tozers' lilacs in the center of the dining-room table. She was eager about this visit. Her last good friend had moved to Arizona four months before.

Promptly at noon, a silver Jaguar pulled into the driveway and Myra greeted the boniest, most elegant woman she'd seen in many years. "I'm Mrs. Box-Smith," the woman said, presenting her name like a hostess gift, "and in sixty-two years I've never known another Myra."

"Neither have I," Myra said, pushing the griping Miss Hyde to the side of her brain.

They looked at each other. Mrs. Box-Smith was as skinny and polished as a pool cue. Her pale hair was rolled back in a French twist, and despite the day's damp heat, she wore a beige cashmere sweater. Her features were upswept and slightly surgical; her smile quivered but never stopped. "You're taller than I guessed," she said. "I admire a woman who can wear pants like she means it."

"Well, my husband's dead," Myra said, surprising herself.

But the odd remark went straight over the smooth head of Mrs. Box-Smith, who was looking around the living room. This inspection embarrassed Myra, who knew that her things didn't fit right. The black Japanese TV atop the worn-out hi-fi—new and old did not look good together.

"Heavens, what beautiful lilacs."

"From my neighbors, the ones who want to use my name."

"Yes, Myra, I want to talk to you about that." Mrs. Box-Smith winked confidentially. "After lunch."

The soufflé turned out especially good, tall and crusty. Mrs. Box-Smith ate like a war orphan. Three helpings vanished down her long throat. "I adore food, especially food that tastes good. When my son Chas was a teenager, he called me Hoover."

"You're lucky to stay so slim."

"I'm forever on the go." Mrs. Box-Smith rapped her knuckles on the maple tabletop and looked around the dining room, settling her eyes on the framed picture of Myra's son, Loren. "It's remarkable how much your boy looks like Jerry Lewis. As a young man, I mean, when he made those funny movies."

What a thing to say! Myra looked at her son's face more close-ly but could only see the little boy who had danced on the sofa and written her funny songs.

Myra said, "I don't see him very often. He lives in France." Outside, the spring sky was darkening and lowering. The Tozer children were shouting in their yard.

"I live with Chas and his wife. They have a big house, so I have my own rooms on one end. It's an excellent arrangement. Myra." Mrs. Box-Smith pushed her plate aside, businesslike. "I have something to tell you."

Myra leaned toward her confident guest, who looked closely into her eyes through contact lenses tinted the bright blue of a postcard sky.

"I should start by saying that my name isn't Myra, strictly speaking. It's Elmira, after Elmira, New York. That's where my parents met. But they always called me Myra."

"I see," Myra said, disappointed.

"They loved me very much. You should love your name for your family's sake, if nothing else. Think what it must have meant to them." Mrs. Box-Smith folded her hands on the table-cloth and nodded.

"I don't know why they gave me this name," Myra said. "I didn't start wondering until a few months ago, and by then there was no one left to ask. Anyway, please go on."

"Well." Mrs. Box-Smith considered. "You are you, and Myra is your name." Her persistent smile tended to flicker a little, like faulty wiring. Could it be that, after promising to help, she had nothing more to offer?

Myra rubbed a grape skin into the tablecloth. "They want to take my name for their child, and they don't know me."

"Perhaps they do," Mrs. Box-Smith said. "They live right next door."

"If they knew me, they would not keep inviting me to church. If they knew me, they would call me by my name. But they call me Mrs. Ritter, and I'm not Mrs. Ritter anymore. And everyone who did call me Myra is gone." She lowered her eyes. "Don't

you ever feel that your name has been used up? Or that it just
weighs too much, sometimes?"

"Not my name." Mrs. Box-Smith's hands did not move from
their neat spot on the tablecloth. "My life is very full."

"Really? What do you do?" Myra intended this question to be
a little spiteful, and, indeed, Mrs. Box-Smith flinched. Myra pictured what her rooms must look like. Expensive blinds, drawn
shut. A mirror. A neat, narrow bed.

"I drive," she said. "I love to drive."

At the door Mrs. Box-Smith pressed Myra's hands between her
own dry palms. "I would love to visit you again, Myra Ritter."

"Maybe," Myra said, surprised. "Maybe we can go out to
lunch."

After Mrs. Box-Smith left, Myra saw an oil patch where the
Jaguar had been parked. She tried to think what Monroe would
have used to get the stain off the driveway, but her brain kept
returning to Jerry Lewis and the annihilated soufflé. Once, on a
city bus, Myra had carried on a twenty-minute conversation
with her seatmate, a sweet-faced girl carrying a hymnal, before
she realized that the girl was out of her mind. Not that Mrs. Box-
Smith was insane. But she was not quite what Myra had hoped
for—a nice, normal friend, someone with whom Myra could be
normal and nice.

Monroe joked about getting shorter every year, and it was
true; each year the ground had pulled him a tiny bit closer. As
his legs shrank, his chest seemed to grow thicker, stronger, filling his red chamois work shirts. He was a shy, busy man devoted to wood carving and World War II books. At seventy-two, he
could still read the newspaper and be amazed by the wildness
in the world.

Their marriage had been a long trance. Was that good?

On the morning of her lunch with Miss Hyde, Myra stood on
her back porch, peeking through the window into the Tozers'
yard. Her washing machine was agitating a load of whites, and
she leaned against it, enjoying the pleasant rhythm against her

stomach. She was watching Ham struggle with a new swing set. He couldn't get it to stand up; the legs kept collapsing. Monroe used to help with these things. Now Ham was on his own.

In the kitchen window, Lisa was washing dishes. She was a large, humming girl who'd married young. Myra had difficulty imagining an inner life for her neighbor. Rather, she pictured Lisa as a lump of warm, rising dough that cheerfully let her family feed upon her. Now Lisa looked up and saw Myra. Smiling, she lifted a soapy spatula and pointed down to her out-of-sight baby.

Myra quickly waved and ducked inside, ashamed to be caught looking.

As she walked down the hot, breathless hallway of Miss Hyde's apartment house, Myra could see elderly women peering like caged chickens from behind screen doors. Their rooms were dark, cramped with the furniture of their former lives.

Through Miss Hyde's pot-bellied screen door, Myra saw a heavy figure struggling to rise from a chair. Softly, she called, "Don't get up, I can let myself in."

The woman sagged back into place. "Suit yourself, Myra Ritter."

In her baggy summer dress and support stockings, Miss Hyde looked much like any very old woman. Upon closer inspection, though, Myra was taken aback by the vibrant, apparently natural blackness of her hair, and the deep circles beneath her eyes.

She said, "It's going to storm again this afternoon. Damn that weatherman."

"Well," Myra said, "it's spring."

"He said sun. Now my feet will hurt all day."

The room was furnished with a cracked vinyl recliner, in which Miss Hyde sat, a straight-backed chair, which Myra took, and two TV trays set with plastic bowls and plates. There were no books, no pictures on the walls. What did Miss Hyde do to distract herself? Myra could only see a rabbit-eared radio beside the bed in the next room.

For lunch they ate chili on rye bread and chicken broth so salty that it scorched Myra's throat.

"The soup got cold," Miss Hyde complained. "And this chili's too spicy." But she ate every bite and cleaned her plate with her thumb. Then she told her story.

Myra was a family name. Miss Hyde, her grandmother, her mother, her cousin, and her niece all had been named after her great-grandmother, a Prohibitionist famous for lurking outside barrooms in a mourning dress. She would press her face to the window and fix her eyes upon the men inside until they either skulked out or turned their backs upon her. Black Myra, they called her.

"And it was always like that with us and men. We could never get along."

"Oh. Well." Myra wasn't sure what to say. She and her friends had never talked about men as a group, only the few specimens they knew.

The women in Miss Hyde's family couldn't help complaining; that's what drove the men away. But there was always so much wrong—the husbands' hats, the suitors' religions. So they lost their men and lived alone, a house full of miserable Myras, complaining about the wrong turns they had taken.

Miss Hyde told her story matter-of-factly, unembarrassed. She thinks I understand because I'm like her, Myra thought. But Myra could not imagine sharing her shortcomings with strangers, or even with friends. Not even with Monroe, although he must have managed to guess.

"My mother always told me that if I didn't sweeten up, I'd end up alone in an ugly apartment. And that's exactly what happened." Miss Hyde shook her head, and for the first time Myra saw her smile, just a little, at her own huge mistake. "I can't definitely say that the name's to blame, but I can't help wondering what would have happened to a Louise or a Dolores."

Miss Hyde looked at Myra with such intelligent, inconsolable regret that Myra could only think of one thing to say: "You are you, and Myra is your name." But these words sounded just as empty here as they had when Mrs. Box-Smith spoke them the week before.

Miss Hyde had turned her attention to the agitated air outside her patched window screen. "Listen," she whispered. The storm was coming.

When Myra left, moist wind was pushing through the hallway, rattling all of the screen doors. The old women sat just as they had been, waiting.

Monroe wasn't sick very long, less than three months, and spent most of that time in a rented hospital bed wedged into a corner of their bedroom. From there he called to Myra, day and night, until her name barely had enough weight to travel around the house. In the evenings he came out and sat in his chair for a little while. Quiet, lost in his body. She could only sit and watch him.

One morning she was on the porch, leaning against the washing machine, when she heard him call to her. She hesitated for a moment, then walked out of the house, down the back steps and into the yard, where a load of coloreds was blowing on the line. It was a chilly October day, and the laundry was still wet, but she took it down anyway, slowly, piece by piece, pajama bottoms, balding towels, faded sheets. She took down everything except Monroe's red work shirt. For a long while she stood on the back steps, her arms full of cold clothes, watching the shirt lift and wave in the wind. When she went inside, he was asleep, holding an empty plastic cup against his chest.

That night, while she was helping him out of his bathrobe and back into bed, he looked up at her and said, quietly, "It's not my fault, Myra." She cried then, for the first time, for all the wrong reasons.

Sometimes she didn't miss him at all.

They would not leave her alone. Mrs. Box-Smith was most persistent, always inviting herself over, forcing Myra into a series of increasingly lame excuses. Once Myra said, "I'd love to see where *you* live," but Mrs. Box-Smith told her that Chas's entire house was busy being decorated for his birthday. Myra began to understand that Mrs. Box-Smith was not wanted at her son's home, but this failed to make her feel kinder. Mrs. Box-Smith's calls became doubly irritating, regular reminders that Myra had not turned out very nice.

Miss Hyde always called late at night, usually after Myra had fallen asleep, to offer more unnecessary information about Black Myra and her namesakes.

By now Myra regretted writing that letter to the newspaper. She had only wanted to send a message to Lisa Tozer and perhaps meet some nice people, but by the tiny act of dipping one toe into the stream of the world, she had become bound to these flawed and dreadful women. Now, too late, she realized that she'd much rather be by herself.

Finally, she resolved to take action. She decided to bring Miss Hyde and Mrs. Box-Smith together. She would invite them to a picnic at the city park. They would hate one another, they would hate the outdoors, they would never forgive her. And that, she hoped, would be that.

Myra herself didn't like the park very much. The softball field, paddle boats, and barbecue pits seemed to demand a more rollicking appetite for fun than she could muster. But she was certain that the other women would have an even worse time there. To ensure this, she fried two chickens as greasily as possible. She left salt and eggs out of the potato salad and bought the palest, hardest strawberries she could find. She excavated her worst tablecloth, a frayed rag covered with printed pineapples and old family stains.

They rode to the park together in Mrs. Box-Smith's coughing Jaguar. Mrs. Box-Smith did most of the talking, telling the history of her car while Miss Hyde stared at the passing view as if it were her own bare apartment wall.

Myra led them to a picnic table between the lake and the softball field. The day was hot, and there were a lot of teenagers around, splashing and shouting in the water, turning their radios louder and louder. Close by, park workers were trimming trees with a chain saw. Myra smiled as she spread the musty tablecloth. "Isn't it wonderful to be outdoors?"

Miss Hyde sat herself down slowly, facing away from the table. She looked up at the low white sky. "It's supposed to rain again."

"Oh, I hope so," Myra said, unwrapping the chicken, which gave off a raw, oily smell. "I love storms. I'm less afraid of nature as I go along. Except for my own body, of course; I have to keep an eye on that. And human nature, which seems to get worse all the time. But thunderstorms, that's the least of it."

"There are so many other things to be afraid of," Mrs. Box-Smith said, with a light laugh. She leaned her hip against one side of the table and picked a chunk of potato out of the salad. "If I were you, Miss Hyde, I'd pretend that the storm was a big show being put on just for me."

"That's conceited," the old woman said.

"One must be conceited to get by in this world." Mrs. Box-Smith continued to forage in the unsalted salad.

Miss Hyde scowled. "Are you going to save any of that for the rest of us?"

"I adore good food."

The lunch was almost as unpleasant as Myra had hoped. Miss Hyde wouldn't turn around to eat but plainly resented every bite eaten by Mrs. Box-Smith, who, nervous at being disliked, ate twice as fast as usual. Hornets dove for the strawberries. Teenagers bellowed and shrieked in the lake. Whenever Mrs. Box-Smith tried to say something pleasant or Miss Hyde tried to complain, the park workers' chain saws chopped up their words.

Myra began to relax, looking around herself with something near contentment. She'd come here with Monroe two summers ago to watch the little Tozer boy play softball. Ham and Lisa had invited them; back then, her neighbors had been easier to tolerate. In fact, she and Monroe had a good time. She got a splinter from the softball stands. That night Monroe tweezed it out of her palm, then kissed the spot, twice, sitting beside her on the bed.

There really was a storm coming. Myra could feel it rustling, she could smell it, delicious with swept dirt. The young people began to leave. The park workers packed up their chain saws and drove away. Myra felt so good being outdoors again that she didn't immediately notice that the other two women were talking to each other.

"He disappeared into thin air," Mrs. Box-Smith was saying, "as men are wont to do. But I live with Chas now, so it all worked out for the best."

Still turned away, Miss Hyde spoke over her shoulder. "And where's your husband, Myra Ritter?"

Myra took a breath, considered. "Dead." She set the word down like a stone, and that's what it was, pure weight. "Liver cancer."

"That's a rotten way to go."

"It hurt him terribly." Again she hesitated, then she decided to tell the truth. Why not? With any luck she wouldn't be seeing either of them again. "And I wasn't always nice. Once I made him ask for a drink of water even though I knew perfectly well that he was thirsty."

"I'm sure he had no idea," Mrs. Box-Smith said, petting her twisted hair as if to calm it in the rising breeze.

"Dying people always know," Miss Hyde said. "Before my mother died she could hear every word we said at the other end of the house. She could smell the candles burning in the Catholic church a block away."

"I want to die alone," Myra said. This was a brand-new thought, which she suddenly, passionately believed. The idea of her last sight being Ham and Lisa Tozer's bland, kind faces, leaning over her, asking, "Are you OK?"—that was unbearable.

"But you have a son." Mrs. Box-Smith shivered, rubbing her thin calves together. "Surely, he'll want to be there."

"He can come after I'm done. I'm going to want some privacy."

"That's the craziest thing I ever heard," Miss Hyde said. "Once you're dead you'll have all the privacy you want."

Delicately, Mrs. Box-Smith asked, "When your husband passed away, Myra, were you at his side?"

"Yes. There wasn't much to it, though. He was sleeping. Good for him." Myra covered her chin with her hand and looked hard at the softball field.

Mrs. Box-Smith started to reach for a berry, then sighed and let her hand fall empty on the tablecloth.

Miss Hyde said, "I'll die alone, but that doesn't mean that I want to."

Mrs. Box-Smith and Myra glanced at each other, helpless, unable to contradict the old woman. The three of them sat in a gluey silence, watching the trees toss their branches. Suddenly, Mrs. Box-Smith cried out, clutching the top of her skull. "Dear God, bird doo!"

The silly euphemism made Myra laugh out loud. "It's just rain," she said, as a splatter landed on her own shoulder.

"That damn weatherman." Miss Hyde hunched her shoulders and ducked her head.

Mrs. Box-Smith began picking up their cups and plates. "We'd better get going."

Myra leaned her head back, letting another warm drop strike her throat. "This feels good."

"Why don't we go back to your nice snug house and play cards?" Mrs. Box-Smith said, looking longingly at the Jaguar in the far-off parking lot.

"I'm going to stay," Myra said.

"Really, Myra, I must insist." There was an exasperated tremor in the well-bred voice.

"Please go ahead," Myra said. "I can pack this up and get home by myself."

"Don't be nuts," Miss Hyde said. But Myra was already walking away, onto the burnt grass of the softball field.

"Myra!"

She looked back. "Please don't make us stay here," Mrs. Box-Smith called. Her hair was coming down, unwinding in a long, confused curl. Miss Hyde was struggling to rise from the bench but appeared to be weighted in place.

"Go!" Myra waved them away. In amazement she watched Mrs. Box-Smith stoop down and fold her skinny self into the space under the picnic table. Miss Hyde pulled the tablecloth over her shoulders and head, glowering under a tent of cartoon pineapples.

The rain was blowing down hard now, the lazy splats sharpening as they struck Myra's arms and face. But she refused to give up. She turned around and walked to the softball infield, easing herself down, knee by stiffened knee, stretching out in the lumpy grass. The rain battered down; she had to turn her head to keep from choking. She knew how foolish she looked, and she didn't care. Maybe they would leave her alone now. Maybe the storm would blow them away, and she'd have some peace.

As her soaked clothes pressed down upon her, she thought of Monroe joking that the earth was pulling him by the legs.

"Myra!"

She raised her head and squinted but could only make out Miss Hyde hunched under the pineapple tent. A corner of the cloth was blowing back and forth over the old woman's face.

Suddenly, Myra thought that if she only turned her head, she would be able to see Monroe, wearing the red shirt, sunk to his waist at home plate. She squeezed her eyes shut.

"Myra!"

The thunder cracked, close and serious now. She imagined lightning striking all around her, knives thrown down by God, marking the outline of her body on his foolhardy earth. And if he missed, and struck her? It wouldn't be the worst thing.

But it would, it would be the worst thing.

She would never be ready, and she would never understand.

Monroe had been ready, at the end, but she hadn't been able to ask him about it. That would have embarrassed both of them. Anyway, what could he have told her? *Myra, it's not so bad.* He had the clear conscience of a good man.

It wasn't true, what she'd said about Loren. She would want him with her, but she knew he'd probably never get there in time.

Myra finally grew so uncomfortable that her thoughts slowed to a crawl. Before long, the rain clouds rolled away. It was hard to get back up; she was coughing, and her pants and sweatshirt clutched her limbs like seaweed. Her shoes filled with water as she stumbled back toward the picnic table.

"Myra! Help me, please!"

A tendony hand was waving from beneath the dripping table. Myra took hold of it and steadied Mrs. Box-Smith as she climbed out from her shelter, dry grass adorning her loose hair. The shoulder of her sweater had torn.

"Well, Myra, I hope you're proud of yourself," Mrs. Box-Smith said, but really she looked proud of herself, flushed and smiling.

"I'm fine. Here, Miss Hyde." Myra helped the old woman disengage herself from the soaked tablecloth and saw that she was clutching a half-eaten chicken leg.

"Is there any salt?" Miss Hyde said.

Exhausted, out of words, they sat together until the sun came out again, hotter than before. Hornets reappeared, doubly insistent, and the heat carried a familiar, needling scent. Could it be? Yes, Myra could see them—lilac bushes, down by the paddle boats, soaked and dragging.

They dropped Miss Hyde off first, each taking one arm to help her out of the car. She grimaced at the seven front steps of her building as if confronting the sheer face of a glacier.

Myra understood now: They would never go away. She'd called them up, and now she had to live with them, and that was that. But it was still difficult to say what she had to say:

"Miss Hyde."

Myra forced herself to look into the old woman's regretful, alert eyes. She said, "I'll come to see you. At the end."

Mrs. Box-Smith reached out and lightly patted Miss Hyde's wet shoulder. "You may put my name down as well."

Miss Hyde stared back at them, apparently weighing the sincerity of their offer. Myra could almost feel the vibrations of the old woman's brain as she strained to form a complaint. But instead Miss Hyde smiled, just a little—at their foolishness? at her luck?—and let them guide her up the rain-slippery stairs.

The next morning Myra sat for a long time in Monroe's chair, leaning back into his old smell and shape. She tried to think about many things but ended up pretending that she was inspecting herself from heaven: a woman neither fat nor thin, rich nor poor, kind nor unkind.

You are you, and Myra is your name. The words still sounded ridiculous, but they were impossible to argue with.

When Myra opened her curtains, she saw black-bellied clouds muscling across the sky. More storms were on the way, according to the Damn Weatherman. Smiling, she walked out on the back porch to start a load of whites. For a moment she stood looking into the Tozers' window, which as always was frantic with activity. Then she fumbled behind the washer for her walking shoes. They'd grown stiff and a little damp. It was hard to bend down to tie them.

As Myra passed the Tozers' house, gingerly moving her feet inside the unfamiliar shoes, Ham galloped out to greet her. His bald head was dewy with excitement.

"Lisa's going into labor, we're leaving in just a few minutes. I thought you'd want to know, Mrs. Ritter."

"Oh. My. Congratulations." Myra struggled with herself for a moment, then decided, Why not just pretend to be kind? Who would know the difference?

"You may call me Myra," she finally said.

Ham grinned and nodded, as if there had never been any doubt, and hurried back to his house. At the door he turned and shouted her name, twice, in jubilation.

"Just trying it out!"

Myra took a deep breath and succeeded in smiling at her neighbor. Then she started walking, toward the hill with the Victorian house on top. By now, she thought, there surely would be some new people inside.

Good Girl

My ex-husband Cord likes giving surprise parties. Not for the party but for the surprise. He'll do anything to make it happen—tell the baldest lie, pick the least likely setting. That's why we're all waiting at an interstate rest stop on this swampy August evening. We're here to help Cord trick his new wife on the night before her twenty-ninth birthday.

God knows where Jolie thinks she's headed right now. Since her party hasn't officially begun, we the conspirators idly mill around the picnic tables, slick with sweat and jumpy from the bugs. The sun is setting in a fruity smear, but nobody pays attention; we're watching the southbound traffic for Cord's old black Triumph.

"An interstate party, that's so different," says the woman next to me. I think her name is Carla.

I say, "Remember my birthday? At county welfare?"

"In the parking lot, after hours, sure," she says. "You were turning thirty. I thought it would be a dreadful party, but it was lovely, really nice."

It *was* a good party, once I looked past the government dumpsters and chained steel doors, and the fact that my husband had thoroughly deceived me once again. There were bamboo torches and catered Cuban food. Cord gave me a bloodhound puppy with a bell around its neck.

Jolie's party also promises to rise above its dubious setting. True, the highway traffic makes us feel a little slow and beside-the-point, and wayfaring families and truckers laugh at us as they come and go. But there's also a pair of twisted oaks, the rough tables have been set with linen and candles, and two golden young men weave among us, pouring wine.

71

I haven't seen most of these people in the three years since my divorce. They're Cord's friends; they treat me with the smiling tact due the victim of a humiliating disaster, someone who's shot herself in the leg or gotten hit by lightning on the toilet. I tell them, "I'm fine," knowing that at least I'm looking good. But I almost didn't come. Cramps, then I couldn't decide whether to bring a date. What would Cord make of Leo, who has a heart of gold and a tooth to match, or Andre, who stutters the sweetest compliments? They would wound his pride terribly.

Of course I came alone.

I haven't seen Cord in two years, but every few months, late at night, he calls me up. He thinks I still have insomnia. He wants to talk about Jolie.

She always sleeps well, he tells me. She's a good person. He says this with the nervous bravado of a high-school debater, and I listen as long as I can. Then I hang up on him, gently.

I've tried many times to despise Jolie: for her too-sweet name, her pony teeth, her college baton-twirling, her cactus business. But whenever I run into her, waiting in line at the pharmacy or idling beside me at a stop light, she smiles as if I'm the one friendly face in the crowd.

Only once have I seen her with Cord. It was right after their wedding; they were standing outside a garden shop, trying to wedge a box into the back of Cord's old car. I wonder, is Jolie always alone? Or does Cord duck when he sees me coming, afraid that I'll catch him looking happy—or maybe unhappy? Some night I'm going to ask him. After all, we're divorced. There's no reason not to be honest.

The Triumph pulls into the rest stop right on time, five minutes past sunset, but Cord and Jolie don't get out. It looks as if she's trying to tell him something. His face is in shadow, but from the intent tilt of his skull I can tell that he's not listening to her; he's inspecting the party. When they finally get out of the car, it takes Jolie a moment to notice the festivities, and even then she doesn't realize they're for her. Finally, Cord growls with mock exasperation and says, "Happy *birth*-day, Jolie." She yelps and hides her face.

She's come from her cactus patch. Her kneecaps are crusty gray beneath her khaki shorts, and her dark curls are bound up like Aunt Jemima's. The rest of us, of course, have carefully dressed to show off our best features. Jolie pulls off her head rag and flees to the rest room to wash. We're all laughing. But I sympathize, too. I arrived at my own birthday party on a pungent cloud of late-afternoon sex and spent the whole time trying to conceal the telltale snarl on the back of my head.

No matter what Cord had been doing, he always smelled of the Swedish cologne he kept in his bottom drawer, out of the insidious light.

He's looking well, a few ounces thicker in the middle. His hair is lighter. Could he be bleaching it? No, he's just more tan. I dodge this way and that for a view of his ass, and I see that it's as flat and tentative as ever. He was embarrassed that he had one; to remind him, I used to sneak up and pinch it.

Jolie reappears with scrubbed knees and brushed hair. She accepts champagne, slips a finger through Cord's belt loop. "She was just telling me how selfish I was," he announces. Jolie looks hard into her glass.

Cord grins as we applaud Jolie's comeuppance. He isn't an especially handsome man, his face is too round and moony, but he gives the impression of handsomeness. It's the way he holds his face. It doesn't just hang there; he holds it.

Abruptly, Jolie raises and kisses his wrist, grazing his watch strap. He ruffles her hair, mussing it again.

He told me what he's giving her. A quilt, because she's always cold. She's shivering right now.

This party improves as the darkness settles. Except for the idling semis and a bass chorus of flushes from the rest rooms, it's hard to tell where we are. Even the pink glare of the parking-lot lights can't obliterate the swollen golden moon. I'm lightly

murmuring and flirting as I move among these not-quite-
friends. Cord is trimming the ragged ends of the party: fiddling
with the tape deck, bossing the waiters, fumbling to relight a
dead candle. His shirt is crisp and white. When we were married, he walked in on me in the bathtub, begged to hear my
dreams, but so far tonight he hasn't said hello. He hasn't even
looked at me.

Cord used to work in the office tower across from mine. Our
windows were a street's width apart, sixteen floors up.
Sometimes on winter evenings I'd notice him watching me
from his fluorescent cube. One night I waved. He dropped his
head and pretended not to notice, but the next afternoon I got
an anonymous basket of ivy and wild mushrooms. That
evening in the parking garage, he stepped out from behind a
Jeep and blocked my path. I gasped, dropped the basket, and
ran. One thing led to another. On our honeymoon he followed
me around with a camera as I sunblocked my shoulders and
braided my hair. One week before our first anniversary, he gave
me a surprise party at a drive-in movie theater that was closed
for the winter. His friends came. We threw snowballs and ate
German food.

I'm watching the waiters, who are urgently whispering
between themselves, when a dry hand takes my elbow. "I'm
surprised to see you here, Brenda."

It's Cord's old friend Bart. He's bright, forthright, chinlessly
pleasant. I say, "I'm surprised I was invited."

"I don't know why I was invited, either." He slaps a gnat on
the side of his face. "I'm sure Jolie's a nice girl, but I really don't
see her that much."

"That's why I came tonight, just to see them together."

Politely, I ask Bart about his own divorce, and he shares the
usual small facts and phrases, worn as smooth as beach glass by
now. My cramps are getting worse, winching tighter and tighter
behind my party dress.

One of the waiters is shouting at the other. "You never think
of me!" he says. Cord steps toward them, but before he can
intervene, the handsomer waiter tears off his apron, tosses it at

the accused, and stalks away. Soon we see him hitchhiking on the highway on-ramp. The remaining waiter swallows a glass of wine and sits down with his back to the party, so stiff with feeling that Cord backs away, twisting his shirt button.

Bart laughs in my ear. "'You never think of me.' Could all the wars of history come down to those five words?"

The button breaks off in Cord's hand. He inspects it, then puts it in his pocket. For the first time tonight, he looks at me. I wave.

To open her gifts, Jolie sits on a stump, Cord's sweater hanging on her shoulders. The presents are the sort of things you give a woman you don't know—candles, napkin rings, potpourri. Mine is next to last. Cord almost drops it when he hands it to her. "Be careful, it's heavy," he says. "From Brenda."

She glances up, surprised to see me, then carefully opens the box. "Oh, my."

"It's a safe," I say. "You can lock it." It's not a big safe, just a small, tough, fireproof box.

"That's interesting," Bart says. "Is it a joke?"

"Thank you, Brenda." Jolie holds the gray weight on her lap for a minute, smiling at me in puzzlement, while Cord tries to hand her the last present, his quilt.

Over the course of my dead-of-night conversations with Cord, I've learned a lot about Jolie. Her father is deaf. She won a statewide majorette competition when she was seventeen, then broke her ankle walking off the stage. She's a genius with cactuses; they fatten and bloom in her care. In the evenings she sits under a hot gooseneck lamp and tweezes the needles out of her hands. She sleeps hard, marching her legs beneath the sheet, while Cord dials my number from his side of the bed.

He says, "She's a good girl, if you know what I mean."

He says, "She loves me."

Cord is pacing between the picnic tables. More things are going wrong with his party. A toilet in the women's rest room won't stop flushing. A semi has pulled up and fixed its headlights upon us. Mosquitoes are attacking in ravenous squadrons, making us twitch and slap ourselves. Worst of all, people are starting to leave.

I can't take it either. I flee to the women's room and find Jolie rubbing at a grass stain on her shorts.

"Were you gardening before you came?" I say.

"No, I was looking for my car keys. Sometimes the dog buries them. But Cord had them."

"So you couldn't leave and miss the party."

"Yes, he had a good reason." She doesn't stop scrubbing at the stain.

"I didn't know you had a dog."

"A puppy, Sam Spade. He's a bloodhound."

"I had a bloodhound, too."

"I know."

Over and over the broken toilet gulps and swallows. We pause and listen, then we both begin to laugh. Jolie blurts, "Brenda, I'm always glad to see you. It's good to know you're there." She touches my hand with one of her cactus-bitten fingers and gives me the same hopeful, weary smile I recognize from our occasional meetings on the street.

We drift back to the shrinking party. "I should leave," I tell Jolie. "I have terrible cramps."

"Me too."

"They get worse every year. So I guess it's psychological."

"No, it's the full moon. That always makes it worse."

We look up. It's rolling high through the sodium light, fat with its latest month-long slice of my life. Cord comes up behind us and kisses the side of my head. "Hello Brenda, you smell wonderful." He puts an arm around Jolie and says, "Didn't I fool her?"

I smile. Jolie excuses herself.

He says, "She's really surprised."

"You fooled her all right. But you should have let her wash before she came."

"I like her the way she is." This is spoken in the same challenging tone he uses when he tells me she's a good person.

"I like her too," I say.

He leans close, offering me the time-warp scent of his Swedish cologne. "You look down on her. She's idealistic. She's superstitious."

"That's all right."

"She's possessive; she goes through my wallet. She's always cold."

"You're not very possessive of her."

"I don't have to be. She loves me."

I let this accusation fly cawing over my head. Up close I can see that he's twisted three buttons off his shirt. A mosquito bite has pushed his cheekbone out of shape. He says, "What was that safe supposed to mean?"

He really doesn't understand, which makes me feel sorry for him, which as usual makes me crabby. "Cord, why did you invite me here?"

"I wanted to see you." I duly note the punitive past tense. "I wanted to see how you're doing. And," he sighs, "I can see you're doing fine."

"I'm sleeping a lot better these days."

"If you're so happy, why are you here?"

Bleakly, we behold one another, as the semis grind in and out of the parking lot and the moon rolls upward, growing smaller and whiter, dragging on me like a magnet.

"What were the waiters fighting about?" I finally say.

He shrugs, folding his arms about himself.

"It's a nice party," I say.

"Jolie should cut her cake now. People want to get going."

"You really surprised her."

He smiles a little. "That's the important thing."

I want to ask, Why? What do you hope to see inside your wife's surprise? Instead, I hug myself and say, "This moon is killing me."

"I know," he says. "Isn't it great?"

The abandoned waiter sweeps dirty wineglasses into a box. He seems to enjoy the pained noises they make. Bart and I huddle around a citronella candle at one of the last lighted tables. We're swapping tales of romantic failure, but I'm only half-listening to him. Mainly, I'm remembering Cord.

I remember his habit of pushing back the thick hair on his forearms as if constantly surprised and revolted to find it there. I remember his Christmas gifts, always wrong, bought in one desperate, last-moment burst: the spangled tights, the ankle bracelet with the tinny, bendable hearts. I remember his back in bed, not the turned back of rejection but the nudging back of a forever bashful lover. I remember Cord's back pressing against me as he tried to burrow out of bad dreams he'd never admit.

When I sneaked up to pinch him, he'd whirl away and press his back against the wall. He would try to laugh.

"There was no one problem," I tell Bart.

But I also remember the day I discovered that Cord had swiped my list of reasons to live. I'd made the list in high school (cocker spaniels, stargazing, etc.), stuck it in an old diary, and forgotten all about it until I found it in Cord's top dresser drawer. I hadn't been prying, just looking for aspirin. Further investigation turned up three snapshots of me, each taken without my knowledge: clipping my toenails, eating salad with my fingers, staring slump-shouldered at my bedroom wall. Me: pasted over with thumbprints and tucked away under old Lotto slips and a never-used passport.

I began locking the bathroom door against his visits. When I moved out, I pretended there was someone else. Every time he called, he begged me for a name.

I tell Bart, "I'm sure we're both better off." But I can't help thinking of Leo's gold tooth, and the way Andre lets his mouth hang open in bed.

Bart says, "He wanted to be married to you."

"That wasn't enough." But I have to correct myself. "It was too much."

The waiter is piling dirty platters into the back of a station wagon. Cord hovers beside him, arguing, pleading, finally offering extra money. The young man shakes his head and keeps noisily loading the car. "This is the worst party I've ever worked," he says.

"Well, you're young yet," Cord says.

The boy laughs, but he leaves anyway.

I watch Cord gather himself together, stacking up his vertebrae, searching the dimness for the woman who loves him. And I realize that I never bothered to sneak through his wallet. There were no secret pictures of Cord, no greedy questions, just me grabbing at his ass, trying to make him hide. To want to steal him, that would have taken a better person than I.

And yet, here I am.

The cake is fluffy and white, too sweet, but we all eat it. "I have to go," I say, to this person and that. Then Cord leans over the tape player, and suddenly there's a blare of marching music. Cord pulls Jolie under one of the parking-lot lights, and with a ringmaster's flourish he hands her a baton.

The cone of light is fizzy pink, a riot of bugs. Jolie pulls back, pleading, but Cord has a grip on her arm and we stragglers are loudly insisting. And Jolie's own knees are starting to work, obedient to the march. She hurls the baton into the night sky.

We cheer, but ironically, and Jolie fumbles on the catch. Cord's big sweater confuses her arms; she pulls it off and tosses it at him. She begins to twirl.

She works hard, wrists straining for control, wrestling the baton behind her shoulders, between her thighs. We honestly cheer her on.

The baton lunges back and forth, muscular, flashing. The music is a blaze of brass, and I can't help it, I'm marching too, just a little, on the edge of the party where no one can see me. I'm whispering, "Don't drop it, Jolie." I'm thinking, Please take it from here.

Now she's scowling, warm at last, pumping her sturdy, stained knees. As the music fades, she gives the baton one last moonward toss, snatches it back, presses it to her heart and bows. Everyone whistles and applauds. Cord spins her in a triumphant circle.

Still frowning, Jolie looks around at the trucks and trash cans. Her eyes wander to the dim fringe of the party and fix upon me. I wave, but she only stares back, holding the baton to her chest.

The music is gone, evaporated. It's gone, but I'm still marching. "It's OK, Brenda," she says. "Stop. You can stop now."

These Things

Charles doesn't really want to watch home movies when he asks about the old projector; he's only making conversation. He's been visiting his parents for three days, and they're running out of pleasant things to talk about. But Charles's father isn't used to idle questions. Immediately, he goes down upon his knees in the hall closet, searching for the box of movie reels, cursing with all the pent-up power of his newly retired throat.

"Junk everywhere I look!" He's found the projector case, but the handle is snagged on something and difficult to dislodge amid the slapping arms of furloughed winter coats. "Damn it, Lois, how could you let it get this bad?"

Charles's mother merely smiles and sets up the card table for the projector. She whispers something to herself. Since her husband's retirement, everything is even more her fault: the confused closets, the musty basement, the tulips that have stopped coming up in the spring. She doesn't seem to mind.

From the rec-room couch, Charles can see his father's struggling back and haunches; his muttering head is buried deep inside the dark closet. Should Charles be helping him with the mess? No, it's his father's vocation. He's a worrier, a weed whacker, an outraged devourer of reports from Washington and abroad. His wife soothes him as best she can.

He shoves a tackle box out behind him, then a Christmas tree stand. "Tomorrow I'm calling Goodwill to come get all this junk. When do we ever use it? Nobody has so much stuff!"

"Everyone does," Charles's mother says, under her breath.

"What, Mom?"

"Nothing, Charley." She draws the rec-room curtains against the overcast afternoon and sits down, waiting for her husband to bring in the projector.

This is the sort of episode, senseless yet tense, that will make Charles angry when he has a chance to reflect upon it, back home in Palo Alto. He will go to dinner parties and complain with everyone else about home, his ill-suited parents, the many mistakes they made. But in fact he doesn't mind being back for this annual August visit to Pennsylvania. He almost enjoys lying on the eternal plaid couch, basting in the damp heat, eating stale potato chips out of a cracked mixing bowl, listening to the familiar gripes and fussing, and, to tell the truth, feeling a little superior to it all. He and his own wife hardly ever argue.

Once his father extricates the projector from the closet, he sets it up with surprising grace and speed. Soon Charles is caught up in sounds and smells, not of memories but of the movie equipment itself—the rattling old machine, the cone of swirling light it casts, the pull-up screen with its warm chemical scent.

The movie reels are disordered, of course, so they watch hit or miss, tugged back and forth through time, from the faded colors of a long-ago lake to the murky wedding of a cousin they never see. "Black and white makes it look like a hundred years ago," his mother says. "It feels like a hundred years ago," his father says. They watch an old post office picnic; Charles's father identifies everyone on film and sorts them into two piles, alive and dead.

Outside the day grows darker and darker and finally collapses into rain. Back in California, Charles always forgets how wet it is here, how damp and shadowy this little house, which like every other house on its street sits in a neat brick square on a neat quarter-acre. It's the house he grew up in.

But he's noticed a few changes, this visit. End tables and kitchen counters have been swept of all trifles; only necessities—a fire extinguisher, framed pictures of Charles, his sister Judy, and their children—remain. His mother has let her hair grow long and silver. She has a new habit of tapping her crossed right foot, marking off the seconds. She seems peaceful, though, as if she finally has time to sit down and let the comforts of faith do their work.

His father has retained the springy, alert body of the working man, but there's a strained look around his eyes, as if he's struggling to see something coming at him from the dark.

They've each done one bad thing.

At eighteen, Judy, the Top Senior Girl, got pregnant by a buck-toothed boy in truck driver training school.

Charles dropped out of Antioch College to sleep days, smoke dope, and sell corn dogs from a pushcart at a Cleveland park.

Their father refused to stand up and say something sweet about his wife at their twenty-fifth anniversary party. When pressed, he turned and walked out of the tent.

Their mother moved out for a month to a phoneless room at the Y.

These are the four bad things of their joint life, all committed at about the same time, no longer worth mentioning since everyone is more or less even. Besides, things worked out. Judy married the trucker, who was quiet and kind and eventually got a better job in computers. Charles went back to Antioch and on to a life of well-paid marketing. Their parents' marriage knit back together into one cranky but solid bone.

Charles knows that, compared with other families' cruelties and disasters, the four bad things aren't really very bad at all. Still, near the end of his summer visits, or during the biannual Christmas trips that he and Judy make with their spouses and children, these things sometimes threaten to come up, simply because they are there. It's to avoid them that Charles does pointless things like ask for old movies.

As far as he knows, there have been no bad things in his own household, so far. But this clean record is itself a pressure that can make him lie taut in his bed in the middle of the night, counting the breaths of his sleeping wife.

Charles's mother pumps her foot, and Charles and his father twist their cowlicks, as they watch Judy prance across this very room, eleven years old, showing off her new book bag.

"Do you have a camcorder, Charley?" His father asks this with deference. He may doubt his son's piety and politics, but he has faith in his mastery of modern life.

"I borrowed one once," Charles says. "Last Thanksgiving. I tried to make you a video." He'd hoped it would persuade them to buy a VCR. But he never sent the tape. Replayed, the turkey had looked wan and puny, misplaced in the brightness of a California afternoon. Evan, ten, stomped around imitating a professional wrestler, and Courtney puffed out her six-year-old stomach and vamped around the holiday table singing "Hit Me Baby One More Time." The worst thing had been his own audible, exasperated breathing, his peevish pleading with the children to behave, to smile, to be themselves. Only his wife, Donna, had come out all right, relaxed, smiling through the camera lens as if she could see her in-laws, lovable and shrunken, on the other end.

"You should have sent it," his mother says. "You shouldn't be such a perfectionist."

Charles stands before them, eight years old, selling ice water from a stand outside the house. Waving pudgy arms, he silently hawks his product to skeptical neighbor children.

"You can hear everything nowadays," his father says.

"Too much," Charles says.

The little boy sets a plate of raw, cut-up hot dogs next to the water pitcher. Charles and his parents fall stiffly silent, reminded of the Cleveland pushcart era. To pull them back to his successful present, Charles says, "Do you watch these old movies much?"

"These old things!" His mother laughs. "Oh, never."

"I'm going to get rid of this whole set-up," his father says. "It's just taking up space."

Charles can hear it in their voices. They're ashamed—for having bought equipment that one day would be obsolete, for having wanted it at all. They've done that a lot, this visit. His mother complained that her sewing machine ran too slowly, and his father denounced his once-sacred riding mower as a rickety piece of crap.

It's twilight-dark on the other side of the curtains, though it's only three in the afternoon. Rain drips from the old oak that leans over the house, adding an extra layer of shadow. Charles pulls his mother's abiding rust-brown afghan around his damp-chilled shoulders, hands another reel to his father. He has two more days here.

It's Christmas Day on the movie screen. Charles and Judy, seven and six, are jumping up and down in a large cardboard box. Behind them the plaid couch is piled with opened presents.

Now, thirty years later, it stings Charles to see the Christmas toys lying ignored. The tea set, the Matchbox cars, the stacks of games—he thinks of his parents buying and wrapping the gifts, then watching as they were inspected and abandoned. He thinks of all the things his parents bought, for their children and themselves, then defeatedly laid away.

"Did you keep those games?" he says.

His mother says, "I think they went to St. Vincent de Paul."

"They're worth a lot now." He sits upright, suddenly urgent. "Could you look, do you think?"

"Anything in that basement is going to smell awful musty," his father says.

"I don't mind. They're worth a lot."

His parents glance at each other, baffled and flattered. His father shrugs and turns off the projector, which winds down with an elderly sigh. "It's a mess down there," he says, but he buttons up his sweater and goes down.

The water came in every summer, seeping through the basement walls, filling the house with the high, insinuating scent of mildew. It was an odd smell, not of nature, not of people, but of nature working on people's things. His parents tried to stop it. They put up paneling one spring, but by July the water had soaked the boards and they had to tear it down. They tried a dehumidifier, which by every afternoon was overwhelmed and dribbling onto the floor. They tried an antifungal wall wash that within a month had sprouted a mural of white blooms. Then they gave up, though they didn't give up complaining about it.

Charles's father is complaining now, below them. Boxes of Christmas decorations are soaking wet, ruined! His wife never helps him! His voice is muffled but unflagging. Charles's mother listens, her head tilted toward the floor; when she sees her son watching her, she smiles.

"You should move south," he says.

"Then who would worry about this house?" She shakes back her new long hair. "Really though, I wouldn't mind moving. Arizona or the Ozarks. Or California."

Before Charles can reply, his father emerges from the basement bearing a damp Go to the Head of the Class game and Barbie's dowdy friend Midge. "That's all," he says. "There was too much to hang on to. It was hard to please you kids."

"It's always hard to please kids," Charles says, diluting the blame. He and Donna selectively buy toys for Evan and Courtney, hoping that this will make them more appreciative, but these things are dropped and forgotten no less heartlessly.

His father holds out a bleeding hand, scratched on the underside of his basement stairs. "There's no end to the junk down there."

Charles says, "Maybe I can use some of it."

"Nah, Charley, Goodwill wouldn't even take it." He waves away his wife, who is pursuing him with a can of Bactine.

Charles insists upon appraising some of the basement inventory. His father goes back downstairs, shaking his head.

"The Carolinas are supposed to be nice, very polite," his mother says. She's pulling open the kitchen cupboards, in case there's something he wants in there. The shelves are crammed with chafing dishes, small appliances, centerpieces, candlesticks. The counters, by contrast, are nearly bare. There's only a notepad and some pill bottles. And the Mixmaster, which his father brought home the night of the twenty-fifth anniversary party, late, after walking out. Not long after that, his mother moved to the Y.

The night she left, his father sat waiting on the front steps, sorting through an old box of coupons. Charles and Judy peeked at him through separate windows.

Charles visited her once during her month away. She wouldn't show him her room. She took him to the cafeteria, and they talked about school. After she came back, she'd corner him and Judy separately, on the stairs or the porch, and she'd embrace them, hard, burrowing. They were gracious about it. They knew they'd be leaving for college soon.

Now he thinks he should force her to explain a few things. But she's so slight in her lilac sweatsuit, standing close beside him, and the truth is that he doesn't really want to know. He takes down a pink glass serving dish shaped like a chicken. It's been broken and clumsily reglued.

"Isn't it awful?" his mother says.

"Where did you get it?"

"Your father won it in a raffle." She twists a strand of her hair, and Charles notices that she's not wearing her wristwatch.

He sets the chicken on the counter, next to the toys. "Donna can use this. Where's your watch?"

She hides her left hand behind her. "I lost it," she whispers.

"How?" he says, more sharply than he intends.

"Ssh. I'm not sure. I've looked everywhere."

"Does Dad know?" He had given her the gold-plated Timex after she moved back from the Y.

She shakes her head. Right then, Charles's father surfaces, perfumed with mildew, holding out a vinyl ice bucket stamped with their family crest, and a lacquered conch shell.

"I'll take those," Charles says, gathering them to his shirt.

"With my blessing," his father says, and he descends once more, unbidden. Soon the kitchen table is covered with his excavations: the *World Book Yearbook* for 1969, a copy of *Profiles in Courage*, Charles's bronzed baby shoes, Judy's Girl Scout canteen.

"You can't possibly want all that," his mother says.

"I do," Charles says. At least, he wants to show that he wants it. He's a little troubled that his father is giving it up so easily—

aren't parents supposed to hold on to things? Every ugly souvenir and memory? Won't he hold on, when his time comes?

His father moves faster and faster on the basement stairs, piling it up. There's a small tin globe, frosted highball glasses, a child's Halloween ghost costume, a wall clock shaped like England. He tries to give Charles a set of twelve silver dessert spoons, but his wife snatches the box for herself.

"They were a wedding present." She carefully pries the box open. The three of them stand with their heads together, looking down at the spoons, nestled in their purple velvet, never touched.

His father sighs. "I just want things to be in order for once."

She puts her hand on his arm. "I know."

Still, she keeps the spoons.

His father packs it all up for him, filling three big boxes. He fumbles with the tape, nicks his fingers, curses all the while he works. Charles sits beside him like a child, watchful but powerless to help. The boxes won't stay closed at first, it takes a lot of squeezing, but finally they stand secure, cinched with crooked yards of tape and old saved twine. Charles admires the boxes, and for the first time this visit, he doesn't feel irritated or superior; he feels protected.

His father pushes the last box away. He stretches out his legs and rests his feet upon it. "I don't mind about the watch," he says. "Wasn't that a whole life ago?"

Charles and his mother quickly glance at one another. Then they too put their feet up on the box. The three of them sit like this for a few minutes, quietly, trying not to smile.

There's too much for him to check through the airline. He carries one box with him, and his father returns the other two to the basement. "They'll be waiting for you next time," he says.

Then Charles is walking up to the little commuter plane, and they're standing on the other side of the cyclone fence that separates the tarmac from the town. They're leaning on the fence, their fingers entwined in the twisted metal. A strong wind pushes against them, blowing their hair back from their skulls. It's the way they lean and watch him, not taking their eyes off him—suddenly, Charles is desperately sorry, even though he hasn't done anything wrong in a long time. He pauses on the flimsy stairs to the plane, and he waves, waves, while the other passengers pile up behind him. Because he doesn't know what else to do, he points to the box under his arm. His father and mother nod and smile and wave him on, and, finally freed, he turns with aching eyes and smacks his brow on the midget doorway to the plane.

His wife and children are happy to have him back. They patiently sit through the opening of the box and even welcome the old things. Donna picks up his baby shoes, kisses each one on its bronzed toe, and ceremoniously sets them on the mantel. Evan, who is wild about the Tower of London and all its ancient terrors, claims the England clock for his room. Little Courtney carries Judy's old canteen to the kitchen sink and fills it.

Soon, though, the children want to go off and play. Charles lets them go. He gathers Peaches the schnauzer onto his chest and stretches out on his taupe leather sofa. He watches Donna stuff a chicken in the kitchen. Her back is smooth and golden; her hands don't hesitate; she's the most guilt-free person he's ever known.

"There are two more boxes back there," he tells her.

"I'll find a place."

That's what he wanted her to say. He lies there a while, warming, relaxing, then he gets up to look at his garage.

He's loved this garage from the day he moved in, even though it's identical to every other garage on the street. He exults in the brightness and airiness of it; he admires the neatly stacked boxes of old newlywed and baby things. The dry order makes him proud. Now, in jubilation, he presses the button that sends the big door upward, throwing his household open to the eyes of his neighbors.

It's a hot, bright, droughty California afternoon. He's just about to stride out into it when he sees, in the center of the concrete garage floor, a puddle of what looks like pancake syrup, embedded with dog hair, two baseball cards, an oven mitt, and a doll's diaper. Glistening bicycle tracks spread the syrup across the floor and down the driveway.

He can't help it, he starts to get mad. To turn their backs on such a mess—to walk away and leave it! He bends down and tries to scrape up the syrup with a piece of cardboard, but it's half-hardened. He drops the cardboard and sits back on his heels, defeated. His head aches from hitting the plane door that morning. He wants to call out to Donna, he wants to shout, Help me!

But he doesn't shout. To have a tantrum on his first day home, that would be a bad thing. Instead, he lowers the garage door and goes into the back yard to calm down.

Courtney is standing on the deck with her tiny nose pressed to the canteen's canvas pouch. "Smell, Daddy." Charles lowers his face and sniffs the cloth.

"What's that smell?" she says.

It's impossible to explain mildew to a child who's only known drought. "It's Grandma and Grandpa's house," he says. Satisfied, she takes the canteen inside, leaving the screen door open. A hornet follows her in.

Unused to the clear cut of light here, Charles squints as he inspects his lawn. Then his eyelids spring open in outrage. The grass hasn't been watered; except for a hundred quick-sprouted weeds, it's brown and shriveled. A week's worth of schnauzer droppings lie scattered and abuzz with flies.

Is this how they prefer to live without him?

He gets a box and a garden glove, and he paces the burned grass, harvesting dog shit. All the while, he's picturing Donna's bare back turning luxuriously in the bed he has vacated. He pictures her sitting with the kids on the living room floor, all three of them with dirty bare feet, close together, eating drippy slices of pizza out of a delivery box. Cobwebs darken the corners of the room, and shingles are drifting off the roof, but they don't care.

Charles stabs at dog droppings, decapitates swaggering

weeds. Before long, his anger reverses direction and drains backward to Pennsylvania.

He used to play in that basement. He used to run laps around the stout old furnace, untroubled by the reek and dampness, the beams full of lounging spiders. Then, in junior high, he began noticing other people's basements, which had paneling and carpeting and TV sets.

Charles stands blindly in his sun-seared yard, replaying old scenes, remembering his parents' share of the four bad things. He stands entranced by resentment, rehearsing a dozen accusations he may one day make.

When Donna calls to him that his chicken is ready, he's rescued and grateful and suddenly starving, but before going inside he pauses to flip a dry piece of dog shit over the fence into the yard of his neighbor, a guy he usually likes.

Later he sneaks upstairs to the bedroom and calls them. It's one o'clock in the morning in Pennsylvania, but to his astonishment they are still awake. His mother gets on the extension, and the three of them chat as if it's four in the afternoon. He assures them that he got back to Palo Alto safely, he describes the meal he got on the plane, but the whole time he's wondering what they're doing up at this hour—arguing about his assorted crimes and mistakes, maybe relaxing now that he's gone?

While he talks, he picks something sticky off the bottom of his shoe. A piece of tape from the box. His father's inky fingerprint is pressed upon it. Charles rolls it up and balances it on his palm.

He reports that Evan liked the clock, that Donna used the highball glasses for dinner, that Courtney took the canteen to bed with her. "But it did smell a little," he says. "Moldy."

"Well, you know how damp it is down there," his father says. His mother says, "It'll dry out in all that nice sun of yours."

Their braided voices, their mild denial of blame, make Charles angry again. He sits upright on the clean beige linen of his marriage bed and says, "Nobody else has a moldy basement!"

He's dismayed by the childishness in his voice and adds a raw half-chuckle so they'll think that he might be joking. He expects they'll either rush to defend themselves—we tried! the dehumidifier, the fungus wash!—or shut up, wounded. But instead they laugh on their separate-but-united telephones, as if he's the sweetest, dopiest kid in the world. His mother's laugh is light and easy, an upward puff, a feather or a spore. His father doesn't laugh that much; his throat's a little creaky, like a startled step in the dark.

"Now Charley," he says, "just let it go."

His mother's voice folds over his father's, wrapping it up. "Yes Charley, why not let it go, now?"

Toys

Holly dreaded the school buses. Their lumbering pace, their flashing red lights, their smug air of entitlement as they inched down the road—the mere thought of these things could taint her day even before she left for work in the morning. Still, she knew that she couldn't avoid the buses, and she'd invented a technique for dealing with them. Whenever she was forced to stop behind one, she made a point of looking away from the windows full of children to the surrounding Berkshires, to the postcard trees and streams and cows. Using this approach, she managed to cope with every bus but one.

Bus 40 was not just slow but malicious. The driver never pulled over to let Holly by and sometimes even veered left to keep her from passing. She found herself trailing the bus at least once a week as it crawled through the hills; often she arrived at the aerobics studio just in time to teach her class. One morning Bus 40 sat in the road with its stop sign out for a full five minutes. Holly had cramps that day, and when the rear-window children pointed and laughed at her elderly Saab, she cried for the first time in years. The following day she gave the bus driver the finger, twice, to make sure he saw it.

Exactly one month later, after waking up to a fresh assault of cramps, Holly left home extra-early, determined to avoid the bus. It was a bright May morning, and schoolchildren were standing along the roadside, dangling their backpacks. Holly didn't realize that she'd slowed down to look at them until a horn bellowed at her rear. She saw that Bus 40 was behind her.

She speeded up, and the bus did too, until its face filled her rearview mirror. Then she saw a dead squirrel lying like a dropped toy in the middle of her lane. She swerved hard, and although she managed to avoid the squirrel, she lost control.

93

Just like that, she was plunging through a ditch full of wild-flowers and bouncing down an incline into a cow pasture. The Saab skidded and squealed, scraping its belly over ruts and rocks, then hit deep mud and stopped with a lurch. Holly pushed open the door, climbed out on shaking legs, and turned around just in time to see the bus roll out of sight.

She stood ankle-deep in the muck, shading her eyes with her hands. A cluster of cows watched her from the edge of the pasture, where they'd fled. Really, though, it could hardly be called a pasture anymore. There was no grass, just a crater of pungent mud surrounded by brambles and thin trees. A bleached barn slumped in one corner, so neglected that its foundation had crumbled away, leaving only rickety stilts.

Was it legal for the bus driver to abandon her like that? She'd never seen him, but she could imagine him: a bitter old geezer with beard stubble, hemorrhoids, and faded Navy tattoos. She probably shouldn't have given him the finger. She probably should have run over the squirrel, but she hadn't had time to think, and instinct had made her swerve.

She tried to start the stalled car, but it had passed out cold—died, probably. Which was no great loss. Years ago, Holly and Jackson had decided to sell the car when she got pregnant. Now the frame was shaky, and rust holes riddled the body. Holly leaned against the driver's door, cradling her cramping abdomen, wondering what to do. There were no houses nearby, only fields and woods. Her aerobic shoes were ruined. Her class was supposed to start in half an hour.

Gnats darted for her eyes and nose. Crows cawed on an over-hanging branch, and the sun burned like a bath of warm vine-gar. Holly had never been the outdoors type and now felt as if somebody—say, her husband's mischievous God—had turned nature up to its highest setting. The cows were coming closer, picking their way over the rocks, curious, it seemed, about the small figure in the spandex shorts and pink hair scrunchy.

She'd never seen a cow up close and was astonished by how patiently they accepted a relentless siege of flies. Their black-

and-white coats were stained with manure and mud. Their empty udders swayed. Who milked and fed them? Cautiously, she reached out and touched the nearest cow on its broad forehead; the animal turned sideways so she could scratch its bony side. The other cows gathered around, staring like refugees over the gaily painted flanks of the Saab.

Two years ago Jackson had covered Holly's eyes with his tough woodworker's hands and, laughing hotly in her ear, led her to the garage. "Wah-lah," he drawled in his favorite joke voice, French redneck, and she saw that each rust spot had been painted over with a sunny yellow sperm cell; the cartoon figures teemed over the car's hood and across its low, nicked sides. Jackson grinned at his own goofiness until he noticed the look on Holly's face. That night he painted over the sperm tails, leaving only yellow dots, which he couldn't resist adorning with happy faces. And Holly had forced herself to laugh.

"It doesn't take a rocket surgeon to figure out why those buses piss you off so much," Jackson said. She'd tried to explain—"It's not what they represent, it's what they are"—but he insisted that her anger was the most significant aspect of the situation.

Jackson himself had never gotten angry, not even during the worst of it, when once a month for six months running he had to produce a sperm sample to be run through a washing device, spun in a centrifuge, then promptly injected into Holly, who waited in stirrups down the hall, boiling with humiliation and unquenchable hope—at these times, her only comfort had been her husband sitting next to her, squeezing her hand and laughingly whispering, "Moo."

Now here she was, surrounded by cows. She wished she had a cell phone so she could call Jackson at his shop. He lived for these moments when life tipped sideways, tossing people about like crickets in a box. Even at forty-one, with worn hands and a weakening back, he possessed a bottomless appetite for foible, pratfalls, irony, and instant karma. He was more or less the same man she'd met ten years before in a porta-potty line outside a Metallica concert.

He'd started out making Windsor chairs and highboys but eventually found that the money was in toys. Now he special-ized in silly things for grown-ups: tie racks with mouse ears, pen trays shaped like spaceships and locomotives. Perpetual Youth, his company was called, and he'd just won a contract to design a line of children's pull toys. Lately, his shop abounded with dinosaur tails, duck bills, and bunny ears, and, really, it didn't bother Holly at all. This, she knew, was progress.

At first she hadn't been able to stand the sight of babies; it hurt to be reminded of what she didn't have. But after the treatments ended, she was surprised to find that babies had ceased to affect her one way or the other. She was equally serene in the face of diaper trucks, her fertile friends, prime-time ads for home preg-nancy tests, and the young mothers who filled her aerobics classes. Only the buses—Bus 40—continued to bother her.

Holly had to admit, real life could be fine. Pressed against her sleeping husband on a warm spring night, in the wide mahogany bed that he'd made, listening to his breath swing back and forth—she didn't need anything else, but she felt enti-tled to more, so how could she help feeling cheated?

The cow leaned into Holly's stroking hands. Through its patchy hide she could feel ribs and dug-in ticks. Could these animals have been abandoned altogether? She imagined the chain of events: the pasture depleted, the milk dried up, the owner dead or flown—

Hard-struck by this thought, Holly didn't immediately notice that the school bus had come back. Then she heard brakes sigh on the road above her. The orange accordion door folded back. The driver sat waiting, but Holly refused to leave the pasture. She stood beside her cold car with her arms crossed, rigid and proud as a prisoner of war. After a few minutes the driver got out. Not an old man after all but a middle-aged woman. She shouted down the incline.

"That squirrel was already dead!"

Holly debated giving the driver the finger one more time but settled for whispering, "Eat shit and die," even though she'd resolved to stop using this expression a few months ago, on her thirty-ninth birthday.

"Do you want a ride or not?" the woman yelled.

The cow nudged Holly with its head. She could have sworn the animal was pushing her toward the road, but there was no way she could sit bleeding and crampy in a bus full of children. She decided to walk home, it was only three miles. Before she left she pressed her forehead to the cow's patient, bitten brow.

Halfway across the mud she realized that she'd hurt her knee. She struggled up the incline, limping and breathless, and saw that the bus was empty.

The driver was heavy and tired-looking, with thick eyeglasses and a T-shirt advertising the town's new heart center. "You knew that squirrel was dead," she said. "What's the matter with you?"

Holly just sighed and got on the bus. The door squealed shut, and with a rumble they started down the road, swaying, jolting, high above the cars that soon lined up behind them. The bus smelled fruity and overripe, like the inside of a lunch box. "I don't want to go to school," Holly said.

"We're going to the garage. You can call for help from there." Both sides of the woman's T-shirt were covered with a drawing of a human heart—the real, ugly kind, with fibrous muscles and dangling arteries. "You flipped me off," she said.

Holly raised her voice above the engine. "Why won't you ever let me pass?"

"You get where you're going quick enough. Don't you? How do your kids get to school?" The woman studied Holly in the rearview mirror, then sighed, shifted gears, and fell silent.

At the garage the woman led Holly past long rows of parked buses, to a phone on the wall of the repair shop. Here buses sprouted wires where their headlights used to be. Their orange hoods were propped open, exposing dark and greasy innards. Holly averted her eyes, first to a calendar page of kittens and toddlers, then to a tray of pliers and tubes, as she waited for Jackson to answer his shop phone.

His answering machine picked up, which meant he was

working hard under a barrage of Led Zeppelin and couldn't be bothered with the outside world. Holly pressed her face against the repair shop wall.

"So I'll give you a ride." She looked up and saw the driver leaning against one of the broken buses, swinging a loose section of black hose.

"I wish I could walk," Holly said.

"We'll take Forty."

When the bus reached the pasture, the driver pulled over, braked, and stood up. "She's all yours."

"What?"

"Try being me for a while."

"I don't want to be you."

"Join the club." The woman sat in a back seat and crossed her arms over the gruesome drawing on her chest. In the pasture cows still clustered around the Saab; the happy faces brightly grinned above the mud. The car had never looked that foolish from the inside, but now Holly blushed—burned all over, her blind heart beating hard—to think of how stubbornly she'd steered it through her town.

She stood up, walked to the front of the bus, and climbed into the vacated driver's seat.

The controls were too big and far apart, and the gears ground in anguish, but finally the bus heaved forward, and Holly managed to keep it moving. "OK, you can pull over now," the driver said, but Holly kept going, ignoring stop signs and honking cars, propelled by a gestating rage, past her house, down Main Street, to the old building by the river where Jackson kept his shop. She pressed the bawling horn.

He emerged cradling a wooden dinosaur. When he saw Holly behind the wheel of the bus, he bent low laughing.

She leaned out the driver's window. "It's not funny," she told him. "The car died. It's dead. Put down those goddamn toys."

The driver was standing behind her, so close that her stale breath stirred Holly's hair. "Did he hear you?" She reached around Holly to flash the red warning lights. "Make sure he heard you."

The Bridle

Not long after she talked Harper into a vasectomy, Mireille decided that she really did want a baby. Harper, a lawyer, argued that a deal was a deal. She dropped the subject, then four months later said, "I'm pregnant," and moved to a pink stucco apartment house on the other side of town.

"Don't let her get away with it," Harper's brother Preston said. "Find another girlfriend right away."

"I want a wife," Harper said. "I want a wife before Mireille has that baby."

He knew this impulse was adolescent and self-defeating, but he decided to give in to it anyway, just for a little while, until he felt better.

Born in Oklahoma, settled in San Francisco, Harper had a long nervous face and thick blond hair that stood straight up, defying his thirty-six years. He wore carefully brushed gray suits and even in casual conversation had a habit of propping out his ears with his forefingers and leaning forward as if wanting to hear. For as long as he could remember, he had tried to be impeccable.

Preston played along with Harper's marriage fantasy, supplying several potential wives. But every candidate proved herself wrong. These women were generous, funny, eager to be wanted. The problem was not with them, Harper knew, but with himself. In despair he withdrew to his work and his apartment, where one closet rattled with stripped clothes hangers and half the walls were bare. He waited for another life to develop.

"Abscess," the dentist said.

"Oh God." Harper cradled his hammering jaw. "How disgusting."

"Hardly," she said, "but it's not surprising either. When's the last time you had your teeth checked?"

He didn't bother answering; it was obvious. Although scrupulous about toothbrushes and mouthwash, he had avoided serious dental work since the adolescent torments of Dr. Dupree's office in Oklahoma City.

"What are you going to do to me?" he asked her.

She dug a knuckle into his shoulder. "Harper, I'm really going to hurt you." Her smile tilted up on the left side. "You need a root canal, right away."

This news made him want to grovel and whine, but her gloved fingers were cool in his mouth, and her breath on his cheek was clear. One of the partners at his firm had recommended her. Harper fixed his eyes on the wall, where engraved jockeys posed in antique frames, and slowly he felt himself unclench.

As far as Harper could tell from his prone position, Dr. Branch was tall and strongly built, with trim dark bangs and peaked eyebrows that made her look unappeasably curious. No sooner had he begun wondering what it would be like to marry her than a rotten smell broke from his mouth. He tried to apologize but only managed to spit on his chin.

"That's the abscess you smell." She pushed a wad of cotton into his jaw. "It's the least of your problems. We're going to be seeing a lot of each other."

An hour later she gave him a roll of cinnamon dental floss and led him to the reception desk. She lingered by the counter as he made his next appointment. "I've never seen anyone do that with their ears before."

Harper dropped his hands from their habitual cupped position.

"Don't stop, I like it," she said. "Not many men want to hear."

When he turned to leave, he walked straight into the coat rack.

Once home, he inspected his tooth, sniffed the fragrant dental floss, and thought about Dr. Branch. There was a slight salt of irony in her manner, as if she'd noticed something ridiculous about him but was willing to overlook it. At the end, talking about his ears, she actually seemed to be laughing at him. On

the other hand, she'd gazed without flinching upon the bad-
lands of his mouth. After great consideration, greater than he'd
given anything since Mireille left, Harper called Dina Branch
and asked her for a date when his root canal was done.

Mireille had never known Harper's teeth were bad. She'd
never even known he was afraid of the dentist. It was so cliché,
so Okie, that he hadn't told her. She only would have laughed at
him, and that was one thing he could not stand. Boorishness he
ignored, insolence he forbore, but mockery left him in tatters.

Mireille was not a beautiful woman, but she wore lustrous
dark dresses that implied a great deal, and she spoke in a murmur so that he'd had to lean close. Usually, what she murmured
was condemnation. Mireille had high standards. Even if she
sometimes was a bit too severe, stretching her contempt to
include dessert, the outdoors, his brother Preston, and eventually sex, Harper knew that Mireille had grasped impeccability.

She had never noticed anything wrong with Harper's mouth
for a simple reason. They didn't kiss. Kissing was one of many
things they lost their taste for during the six years they lived
together. Fragrant flowers, seafood, popular music, figurative
art—it all gradually became intolerable. They weren't unhappy,
really, just refining themselves. Their apartment, subtly stained
and full of dust, began to chafe them. They redecorated in white,
but their relief was short-lived. Dirt showed up worse than ever.
Sometimes Harper caught Mireille looking at his very flesh with
disapproval. When she suggested the vasectomy, he'd seen no
reason to argue.

He didn't regret the procedure. The thought of babies made
him weak, like a near-miss car crash. But in the months after
Mireille left, Harper often found himself lying awake at night,
confounded, wondering how such a fastidious woman could
have come to think that she wanted the mess of a child, and
rooms in a pink stucco building.

Harper and Dina Branch went for a Saturday walk in Golden
Gate Park. It was her idea. He hadn't made any suggestions

because all first-date possibilities, from restaurants to movies, seemed too hackneyed to propose.

The April day was sharp and blue, with a soft gold center. Dina wore a tweed jacket and a tall pair of boots. She knew the park well, much better than Harper, and she led him through gardens and game fields he'd never seen. She walked fast, on springy legs. Harper managed to keep up, but his neck felt stiff and sore, as it always did when he thought he was being inspected.

They walked past windmills and waterfalls and a herd of morose buffalo; they took a shortcut through some woods and discovered a pile of horse manure as tall as a house, steaming in the sun. Harper held his nose and fled into the trees as Dina bent over laughing at him. The manure didn't bother her a bit. Nothing did. Can eyeballs chew? That's what it seemed like as she walked beside him, turning her head from side to side, tasting everything like a greedy party guest. "I'm a perpetual tourist," she bragged.

"Ah," he said, not sure if he liked this.

They paused to rest at Lake Byron. That's what Mireille used to call it, the pond with the mopey willows and fake Greek ruins. They sat on a concrete bench that had been poured to look like marble. "I love this spot," Dina said. "Once I took a picture of those columns in the fog."

Harper rubbed his tense neck. "It's a little hokey, don't you think?"

She studied him. "Are you still upset about the manure?"

"Of course not. And I wasn't upset, just a little disgusted."

"You really take things personally, don't you?"

"Not at all," he said, feeling his ears start to simmer.

"You do! You were embarrassed that I saw you see it."

"That's ludicrous," he said, but his ears were at full boil.

"Yes, Harper, that pile of shit sure made you look bad." Gleefully, she slapped her thighs. She nudged him, confidentially lowering her voice. "But I'm the queen of silly fears. Want to hear?"

"No, I don't." He pretended to shiver. "I mean, we'd better go, it's getting cold."

This was true. The summer fog had come early that year, muscling in from the ocean each afternoon, complicating, every time, what had been a nice bright day.

They went to movies and art galleries; they shared pasta and ice cream. "We aren't missing a single cliché of urban dating," Harper said. "No," Dina said, "and tonight there's Mozart." The Jupiter Symphony, for God's sake. But when Harper saw that no one was laughing at them, that no one even cared, he began to enjoy himself. He liked being pulled in Dina's wake. Neither he nor Mireille had pulled each other. Usually, they'd stayed in.

Dina told Harper about her big New England family and about her ex-husband, the self-centered history teacher, though Harper preferred to change these subjects before they got too sad or intimate. He told Dina about Oklahoma's Baptists and heat and dust, and about his escape to Stanford Law School. He told her about Mireille's baby, due in three months. He didn't tell her about the vasectomy or his not-quite-abandoned plan to get married before the baby came. Indeed, in idle moments Harper still was in the habit of mentally arranging a small chapel wedding that starred himself and sometimes Dina.

Citing professional ethics, Dina referred Harper to another dentist in her office. The reclamation of Harper's mouth was a lengthy process, and often while he was in the chair she sat on a stool behind him, watching. Later, when they were alone, she'd pull apart his jaws to inspect the progress.

In bed she had a tendency to handle him, like a doctor, but she also was affectionate and honest.

"I get shyer as I get older," she said their first night together, at her house.

"Me too." It was strange but not unpleasant to admit this. "I wonder why."

She pressed her leg against his. "I guess I no longer believe that sex can change my life."

"Maybe we already know what we need to know."

"Fat chance." She reached over, turned on the bedside lamp and closed her eyes. Astonished, Harper watched her slide directly into sleep. For the first time, he looked about her bedroom.

Lots of lace and flowers, nothing vulgar, exactly, but nothing that would have passed muster with Mireille, who liked to keep things spare. His eyes skated over baskets and bracelets and perfume bottles, stopping, finally, on a framed charcoal sketch on the far wall. It was the clumsy sort of portrait drawn by the sidewalk hacks at Fisherman's Wharf, and it was of Dina. Her tilted smile had been straightened out, her peaked eyebrows flattened to a magazine blandness. Harper pulled the covers over his chest, staring, unable to reconcile this caricature with the bright and forthright woman who had drilled his teeth.

Now, sleeping, she rolled toward him and took hold of his thigh. He studied her real, complicated face for a moment, then reached over and switched off the light. But when he woke up a few hours later, she'd turned the lamp back on, and the portrait was still tritely smiling at him.

Preston called to announce that he was buying a LeRoy Neiman painting and to invite himself to dinner. He wanted to meet Dina.

Harper loved his brother above all humans, but he knew that Preston's Rolex, nose job, real estate jargon, and leather wardrobe made a certain impression. For two months he had managed to put off introducing Preston to Dina, but now blood loyalty won out, and he invited him over the next Saturday night.

Then Mireille called, for the first time since she moved out. "You wouldn't know me," she murmured. "I'm huge and slovenly. You'd be ashamed to be seen with me."

She said this so proudly that he had no choice but to lie and tell her that he was deeply in love, though he was at best only halfway there. He hinted that he was on the verge of a major commitment.

"I'm very relieved to hear that," Mireille said. "Wouldn't it be extraordinary if you had someone to marry by the time I had my baby?"

It was only after he hung up that he realized that he hadn't asked her the most important question, which still perplexed him whenever he gave in and thought about her and the baby.

Why?

The charcoal portrait and the unquenchable lamp weren't the worst things in Dina's room. One night while Dina was taking a shower, Harper pulled open the drawer of her nightstand and found, amid the tissues and lotions, a small stack of cards, each printed with a different inspirational saying.

Time Heals

All Is Forgiven

He ignored his first reaction, revulsion at her bad taste. Harper certainly had his own cache of things he didn't want anyone to see. But the cards made him worry. Had something bad happened to Dina? Maybe the selfish history teacher had hit her. Maybe she'd been some kind of addict or tried to kill herself. She'd often hinted that she'd suffered a bit before.

But just as he couldn't make himself ask how she had suffered, he couldn't ask about the cards. For one thing, it was nosy. For another, he'd had enough of victims. It seemed that everyone in San Francisco was recovering from one affliction or another, and the melodrama of it all offended him. Who didn't have a bag of sad stories? Maybe Harper didn't have outright tragedies, but he'd had his share of regrets and embarrassments. Probably more than the average person. Sometimes dawn found him rolling back and forth in his bed like a man on fire, tormented by stupid things he'd done in high school.

The fact was, he didn't want to know Dina's gaucheries and misadventures. He liked her strong, ordering wine, parallel parking. Not wounded and taking cheesy solace.

Still, he got into the habit of reading the cards, one each night he stayed with her, always waiting until she went to the bathroom, then sliding the drawer open.

You've Made It This Far

Right Now Is All You Have

∞

Harper told Preston to bring a date to dinner, but as usual he came alone, bearing champagne and supermarket roses, wearing a cashmere sweater patterned with spermy squiggles. He winked at Dina as he grasped her hand.

"Finally," he said. "Harpo's been hiding me."

"I thought he was hiding me," she said.

Preston was two years younger and two inches shorter than Harper. He had the same stiff blond hair, but plastic surgery had demolished the broad bridge of the family nose. He'd never liked Mireille—rather, he knew that she didn't like him—so now he took a double shine to Dina. As Harper peeled and chopped and anxiously eavesdropped in the kitchen, his brother and girlfriend sat on the white sofa, drinking martinis and laughing about him.

"I can't believe you date a guy with teeth like his," Preston said.

Dina said, "I think of him as a work in progress."

At first it had bothered Harper that Dina was so amused by him. He thought it was the same as being laughed at. But he'd come to understand that her amusement was fueled only by affection. That, and curiosity. Sometimes he awoke to find her studying him, eyebrows raised, as if he were an interesting exhibit.

By the time Harper served dinner, Preston and Dina were quite drunk and talking about equity.

Preston said, "I've been trying to convince Harper to go condo, but he can't find anything that suits him."

"They're so cheap," Harper said. "Just plaster and cardboard; anyone can hear anything."

Preston loaded his fork with potatoes. "If you want to see cheap, you should see Mireille's new place."

Dina softly glanced at Harper, who picked a rusty piece of lettuce from his salad.

Preston said, "I drove by one day, just out of spite. North view, no garage, pink exterior."

"The meat cooked too long," Harper said.

"She hated me," Preston told Dina. "And I wasn't crazy about her."

"She didn't hate you," Harper said, wearily. "Should I slice more bread?"

"She called me a 'lackey of Mammon.'" Preston repeated the insult in a nasal monotone that mocked Mireille's fetching murmur. He grinned, lifting a lamb chop with his fingers. "She was right, but still."

From there the conversation progressed to cell phones, street crime, dental bonding, the summer's uncommonly thick fog, and, inevitably, Harper. Preston remembered many funny things about his brother, including the time in seventh grade when Harper sat in chewing gum and was too embarrassed to go to the nurse and get it scraped off. He wore the pants all day; at the end of every class, he'd wait for the room to empty, then scuttle down the hall with his back to the lockers.

Dina squeezed Harper's knee. He got up to clear the table.

Soon Preston was telling how he and Harper used to get picked on by the other boys.

"I still don't know why; we weren't any uglier or stupider than anyone else. The only thing I can think of, our father was dead. No coffee for me, Harpo. For some reason they liked to make fun of our house, even though it was just a regular house. I would always tell them, `It's a six-room house, the same as yours.' And Harper would say, `It's the cleanest house on this street.'"

"It was," Harper said. "Mother never stopped cleaning." But he wanted to change the subject; Dina was gazing at him with bleary, dreadful compassion.

Preston said, "She had big plans for us. *She* needed dental work. She was missing a tooth right here." He tapped a canine. "When she died, we had one put in."

Harper stabbed a fig. "Can we talk about something less maudlin?"

Preston flipped a spoon at him. "What's wrong with you?"

"I'm sick of sad stories."

"What's so sad? But that's a good idea." Preston turned to Dina like a smarmy talk show host. "So, Dr. Branch, what's your tragic story?"

She paused to consider, looking flattered and shy, like an

understudy finally called upon to say her lines. Harper imagined sad tales hanging in her brain like pretty dresses.

"My tragic story. Well. My husband left me—"

"For another woman," Preston said.

"Worse."

"For a guy?"

"Worse! He left me because he wanted more time to read and
play his guitar. Seriously. That's what he told me. Isn't that the
saddest thing?" Preston burst out laughing, and even Harper,
who'd never heard this, had to smile. "I'd stop by his new place,
and there wouldn't be a trace of other women, just his history
books and his guitar, lying on the bed."

"I've seen some guitars with a pretty cute shape," Preston said.

But Dina had stopped laughing. She slouched in her chair, her
eyes on the far wall of Harper's living room. "So I went a little
crazy. Nothing really bad, like slashing his tires. Just embarrass-
ing things, phone calls, crying. I stole his *Lewis and Clark Journals*
and tossed them out in the park." She turned to Harper. "You
should get a picture for that wall, it's too bare."

"He had one," Preston said. "She took it. A big ugly gray
thing. What was it called, Harpo?"

"*The Bridle*," Harper murmured.

"I knew it was something pretentious. Anyhow, she did him a
favor."

"Hey." Dina sat up in her chair, alert again, roused from her
bad memories. She waved a finger between Preston and Harper.
"You two are dressed the same. I mean, the same colors."

Indeed, Harper's black vest and red-checked bow tie mirrored
the colors of Preston's sweater. They stared at each other for a
moment in mute surprise, then Preston resumed his interview
of Dina. "So why you go out with this Okie?"

"He has terrible teeth, no question. But his ears!" She cupped
her hands in imitation of Harper, who smiled at her with what he
hoped was good humor and stood up to blow out the candles.

He offered to drive her home; she wanted to stay.

Getting ready for bed, he said, "Preston's a little flashy."

"I enjoyed him. He's not like you, but he's like you."

"Not much like me."

"You have the same goofy dignity."

Harper chose not to pursue this. He climbed between the sheets. He watched Dina clumsily remove her bra and fling it onto his dresser, knocking his keys into oblivion. He wondered if maybe tonight, since she was drunk, he could turn off the light.

"Anyway," she said, "if you want to talk about mortifying family members, you should meet my brother. He can't get through a Sunday dinner without picking a fight with someone, usually with me. He can start out talking about anything, opera or politics or grammar, and he always ends up throwing his plate on the floor. But you know what's worse? My husband never once got mad at me." She stood before Harper, naked but for her pantyhose, weaving a little, eager to confide.

Maybe it was the winey odor of this offering, maybe just the candid display of pantyhose, which Harper considered the ugliest garment ever designed. But he was unmoved.

She said, "I could go on and on about Ed."

"Frankly, I'd rather you didn't." He switched off the lamp. But he'd overestimated her drunkenness. She turned the light back on, examining him with narrow eyes. She was no longer amused.

The next day Harper was hung over and Dina claimed she wasn't. She wanted to go to Golden Gate Park.

It was the black, windy heart of summer, but despite the weather the park was full of picnics, and parking was scarce. Dina knew that Harper hated to park, just as she knew he hated the fog. He could only assume that he was being punished for not wanting to hear about Ed the night before.

Dina was looking for something called "A Festival of Pakistan," but they walked and walked and couldn't find it, and no one seemed to know anything about it. So they went to an outdoor art show that featured many impressionistic renderings of cable cars and fishing boats. It reminded Harper of the charcoal portrait of Dina and made him feel even worse. "This is horrible," he said. "And I'm cold."

Dina crossed her tweed-covered arms. She tapped her riding boot. "Then let's go to the aquarium."

"I'm not up to fish today," he said.

"Why not?"

Harper bit his bottom teeth and glared into the fog.

She was unrelenting. "Let's go to the art museum."

"Damp, pretentious strangers, just what I need."

They drove back to Dina's house and went to bed. They didn't touch each other, they just pulled up the covers and closed their eyes. It was afternoon, but Dina still turned on the lamp. A few hours later she cried out. "What?" Harper said, meaning, Why are you awake?

"I think I killed somebody, an old woman. You were there too. I said, `What are you going to do, Harper?' and you said, 'I can't hear you, it's too dark.'"

She was sweating, trembling, her damp bangs pushed up in spikes. The room was too hot. He pushed the sheet down to the puckered band of his boxer shorts. "That doesn't make sense," he said.

The charcoal portrait was smiling on its dim wall, but Dina was frowning very specifically at him. She said, "If you were at all curious about my dreams, or anything in my life, you'd know that it does make sense."

He said, "If you kept that light off, you'd sleep better."

"I have good reasons for wanting it on."

"You should have outgrown them by now."

She gave him a sideways, shiv-like look. "Stop that."

"What?"

She jabbed at her ears. He uncupped his own, let his hands fall to his perspiring sides. He watched a pudgy spider sneak across the ceiling. After a minute he said, "You know, I was going to ask you to marry me."

"What?" She sat up, bunching the sheet around her breasts. "When?"

"A few months ago."

Her face fell wide-open with confusion, then pulled back like a rearing horse. She bounced out of bed and into the bathroom, slamming the door behind her.

Vulgar, to employ such a Hollywood gesture. Mireille would have elegantly glided out of the apartment, leaving him to stew for a day or two before returning with a tight smile and no explanations whatsoever.

Mireille had never hounded him with her traumas. She'd had too much pride and dignity for that. She'd been a rare thing, but she was gone now, lost in mad animal dreams of mothering.

An angry faucet was blasting in the bathroom. Harper slid open the drawer of the night stand.

Forget Yourself

Heavily, aching in each of his unfixed teeth, he pulled himself out of the sheets, got dressed, and left, quickly, before Dina could come out of the bathroom.

In the gusty street, garbage cans were tipped over and rocking back and forth. Harper set them upright, three of them, but they'd blown over again by the time he reached the end of the block.

One week after the fight with Dina, a week of cold sores and insomniac housecleaning, Harper got a call from Mireille. She'd just come home from the hospital, with a baby girl. He congratulated her, impeccably. He promised to visit her that afternoon. Then he went to see his brother.

At noon Preston was just getting up, wandering around his chilly condo in a satin boxer's robe. His pale hair was flat and defeated. "Bad night," he said. "Tequila. I got slapped. And she was ugly, too."

Harper took his usual seat, a black leather chair that reminded him of a gorilla's palm. He swiveled back and forth, looking at his loafers. "Mireille had the baby," he said. "A girl. And me not even engaged yet."

"Ask Dina."

"I think we've broken up."

"Shit, Harpo." Preston rubbed his crushed hair. "I'll make coffee."

While Preston banged around his narrow kitchen, Harper pulled up the living room blinds and looked down on the pool area of the condominium complex. Though the Sunday afternoon was clanging with sunlight, no one was swimming. In other windows Harper could see people bent over desks and computer screens.

Preston handed Harper a mug printed with his name, face, and realty office. Harper said, "Too bad that pool is going to waste."

"No one ever goes in. I went down once, but I felt stupid."

Preston sat on a Z-shaped stool made of black metal. He jutted his chin at the wall. "So what do you think of LeRoy?" Harper examined the new Neiman painting. The Kentucky Derby, all legs and sparking hooves. He tried to appreciate the energy, but it was so crass and literal that he couldn't think of a single positive thing to say about it. Finally, he said, "It's very lifelike."

Preston snorted into his mug. "OK, you hate it. But being a lackey of Mammon and all, I like something I can make out."

Harper and Mireille had bought *The Bridle* near the end. It took up most of one wall. They used to lie on their reupholstered white sofa and try to find the bridle in the black and gray slashes. One day Mireille announced that she could see it, a bit and reins, right in the middle of the canvas. She was upset that Harper couldn't see it too. That was right before she decided to have a baby.

Preston said, "I'm thinking of getting a cat."

"Dogs are better."

"Except you have to come home to feed them."

"It's true, you can't be so self-centered," Harper said.

"What's wrong with being self-centered? If there's no one else, who do I hurt?" Preston stretched out his skinny legs and yawned. "And how am I any different than you?" The phone rang. Preston picked it up, listened for a moment, smiled, rubbed his eyes, and said, "Cathedral living room, four bedrooms, four baths."

Back home, Preston had always smiled when the bullies cornered them, a nervous, deal-making smile. Harper tried to argue with them, on grounds of fairness and decency. Later, in the safety of their own house, the brothers would always find a reason to punch each other.

Now Preston piled up money, while Harper piled up spotlessness and pride.

You have the same goofy dignity.

Harper jerked back and forth in the gorilla palm. His neck ached; his knees were twitchy; he wanted to move around. He wanted to go swimming. He decided to suggest it when Preston got off the phone. He'd say, "It's the first warm day all summer, who cares if we look stupid?"

But Preston was deep into assessments and square footage. "Super. Great." He covered the mouthpiece. "Sorry this is taking so long, Harpo, but it's a four-toilet deal."

"Never mind." Harper stood up and poured more coffee for his brother, who was hunched over the table, jotting numbers on a personalized notepad. He dug a knuckle into Preston's shoulder and took one more look at the empty pool. Then he left to see Mireille.

Tiny scraps of clothing, plastic toys, and unassembled crib pieces all sprawled together on the stained carpet of her new apartment. The air was hot and milky. Harper tried not to look shocked by the mess or by Mireille's new short hair and frankly miserable face.

"I'm so relieved that you're here," she said. A flossy-headed baby hung in a pink sack around her neck. "I came home this morning, and I panicked. The future was overwhelming." Her words were rushing out as if he had the only ears in the world. "It's exhausting, Harper. I think of all the schools and playgrounds and emergency rooms, everyone watching and judging me, all the mistakes I'm going to make—"

"Where's the father?"

"There was never a father, just a donor. I should have told you that before. I meant to. Here." She handed him the baby.

The infant curled on his arm like a hot red snail, eyes shut, sunk deep inside herself. "Victoria Alexandra," Mireille said.

"A big name."

"It took me so long to decide." Mireille was bent over, panting, picking up the scattered baby things and tossing them onto the brown velour sofa. "What a revolting mess," she said.

"Babies are supposed to be messy." This one, the first he could remember holding, was surprisingly dense and trembling like an engine.

"It's dreadful, I can't bear it." Chin wobbling, she kicked a box of diapers across the rug. "But I'm trying, Harper, I really am. Because this is better."

"Better than what?"

She sat on the sofa, studying a bulb-headed Tweety Bird doll, not looking at him. "We were choking there," she said. "You must realize that now."

He tried to smile. "Now I choke all by myself."

"Harper." Mireille dropped the toy and reached out to him. "I'll take her."

Harper thought he'd be relieved to hand back the baby, but he only felt a chilly absence. He put his hands in his pockets and walked around Mireille's small living room. He recognized a few things from their former household, looking effete and out of place here. The bridle painting was leaning, huge and gray, against the fireplace.

"Remember how much we slept? Remember our backs, how they hurt every night?" This was the murmur of lost Mireille, but when he turned to her, he saw only a frightened woman with a baby.

"You don't seem happier now," he said.

"Happy." She shrugged. "That's a vulgar little word. This is better."

"This is a truly ugly building."

"From the inside it's not so bad."

Her body was hard to make out through the baggy dress. He gazed at it with fond nostalgia, as at a passing beloved landscape. She said, "Do you want that painting back? I don't have room for it here."

He wondered what Dina would make of the dark ridges and smears. He imagined her leaning over the canvas, trying to pick out the bridle. She'd find it right away. She wouldn't like it—too murky, too gray—and she wouldn't want to look at it for long, but it wouldn't frighten her.

The frame barely fit into his car.

By the time Harper got to Lake Byron, it was cold and getting dark. He knew it was dangerous to go there so late; he could be robbed or, more likely, trip in the dark, splitting his own head open. He crept over the grass cautiously, squinting in the dimness. He sat on the fake marble bench.

Forget Yourself, the last card had said.

Never. Never for a moment—not walking, not working, not listening to Mozart or deep inside a woman—had he been able to forget himself.

But now, as the chill crept through the seat of his pants and his teeth began their twilight ache, he tried.

He pushed out his ears and concentrated, on the shivering eucalyptus, on the splash of invisible birds. Close by, he knew, Buddhas meditated behind museum glass and a mountain of horse manure sat steaming.

Dina was right that first day when she told him he took life too personally. He should know by now that life was content to let him pass by unnoticed.

He tried to keep his mind on the park, but he kept seeing himself. Putting on his best suit, his staunchest suspenders. Knocking on Dina's door. Pulling her outside, leading her to the park, this very bench. He would get down on bended knee, no matter who was watching. He would take her hand, look deeply into her eyes, and ask her to tell him something bad.

The Years in Review

Carrie had lived in the new house for two days when she found the box of pink trash bags under the basement stairs. Immediately, she ran up to the library to show Hal, who was unpacking his reference books. They laughed together, crouched amid stacked chunks of encyclopedia, passing the box back and forth.

"You have to assume that a woman who buys pink garbage bags holds somewhat unrealistic ideas about marriage," Hal said. He enjoyed evidence of other people's foolishness, as if a higher balance of stupidity in the world could only make him smarter. Carrie knew she was the same way.

"Scented bags," she said. "No wonder they split up. Though I suppose he could have bought them."

Hal didn't bother to answer; he'd just found his box of *Britannica* yearbooks.

Carrie and Hal were moving into what their real estate agent had termed "another divorce house," and the failed marriage that preceded them had left a slight smell of ashes. Carrie could not look at the deep Jacuzzi in the bathroom, or the eager ice dispenser on the refrigerator door, without feeling pity and a little contempt. She and Hal disdained divorce as unimaginative and overly idealistic—tacky American, like Lotto or hair transplants. They'd been together for twelve years. "We're in it for the long haul," they liked to say.

The trash bags made Carrie's hands smell powdery, like babies or well-tended old people. She worked in market research, interviewing focus groups about consumer products, and was always interested in new fragrances. Sniffing the box, trying to decode the pink scent, Carrie tiptoed around the columns of books Hal had erected on the library floor. It wasn't a real library, though, just an extra bedroom with hearts-and-ribbons wallpaper that they planned to steam off in the spring. Now it was January; snowflakes as big as butterflies were blowing against the windows, clotting in the screens that the previous couple had neglected to take down.

Hal was struggling to wedge the *Britannica* annuals onto the shelves they'd moved up from the city. Carrie smiled at the back of his neck. "We should pack those yearbooks away again," she said. "We never look at them."

"They cost a fortune. And you know as well as I do that the moment we get rid of them we'll suddenly need to know what happened in—" he glanced at the spine in his hand—"1989."

"I can think of one thing."

Blankly, he looked at her. Then he grinned. "Oh, that." They'd gotten married that year. He tossed the 1989 yearbook onto the crowded floor and wiped his dusty palms on his pants. "This is not a book-friendly house."

They'd hoped to buy something older, with high ceilings and history, but all they could afford was this rectangular ranch house with shallow closets and truck-driving neighbors. The agent had told them, "In this particular market, even professional people have to start out buying blue-collar. It's ironic." He'd intended the word to soothe Hal and Carrie, and it had, for a moment. And the house did have a few nice touches, like the Jacuzzi, although the big tub cramped the bathroom; already Carrie had stubbed her toe on it twice. They had both taken three days off from their jobs to move in, but it was already clear that the new house was too small for all they owned.

Hal reached up, clamped his skull between his hands, and twisted it until his neck cracked. As always, Carrie flinched and looked away. He said, "What should we do about dinner?"

"I bought a chicken. Maybe I'll make curry. If I can find anything to cook in."

But at the end of the day, she was too tired to look for the right pans and spices. They drove through the snowstorm to an Indian restaurant, then came home and crawled yawning and achy into their sleeping bags. They still hadn't set up their bed.

∽

By the time Carrie and Hal went back to work, they'd managed to open up most of the boxes, but they hadn't actually moved into the house. Refugee summer clothing huddled in the corners of the bedroom; displaced utensils crowded the kitchen counters. They'd dragged their mattress into the bedroom and spread the sleeping bags upon it, lacking the time and energy to cope with the box springs and sheets.

It was impossible to get anything done during the week. They worked too hard and too late, and didn't get home until after dark. The first Saturday, they made a point of getting up early. They drank their coffee quickly, standing up in the cold kitchen, then Hal disappeared into the library with a roll of trash bags. Carrie pulled a box of blankets and sheets to the linen closet and tipped the contents onto the floor.

She wasn't sure why she kept saving the daisy pillowcases from her college dorm room or the brown plaid sheets from Hal's bachelor years. Or the mistakes, like the Egyptian cotton sheets that had turned out to be too small for their bed. Standing in the dim hallway of her new house, Carrie was forced to admit that she and Hal owned only two sets of usable bed linen.

Frustrated, she started wadding things up and jamming them into the closet. On the top shelf her knuckles struck something cold and hard. She pulled down a piece of Bible-shaped ceramic pottery stamped with the golden words *Our Special Day, June 6, 1994, Deidre & Steve.* There was a little reservoir for a bouquet, and an empty picture frame.

She climbed over the scattered books in the library and showed her discovery to Hal.

"How sweet. I have just the place for it." He stretched open the mouth of the bag he'd been stuffing with packing paper.

Carrie hesitated. "What if she forgot it?"

"You think she just happened to leave it behind?"

"It seems wrong to throw it out."

"Sweetie, this is a *divorce* house." Hal stepped into the trash bag, pulled the plastic up to his hips, and marched in place to stomp the paper down.

She said, "It wasn't always a divorce house."

"No, I'm sure it was all thresholds and birdies, once upon a time." He smiled at Carrie as he climbed out of the bag, a wad of packing tape stuck to the leg of his Saturday pants. "I hope the suburbs aren't getting to you. I hope I don't come home one day and suddenly find you being a wife."

"Making wreaths, ironing your shirts . . ." Carrie batted her lashes and crossed her eyes.

"Then I'll have to ditch you like what's-her-name."

"Deidre." She held up the little wedding shrine for him to see.

"Dee-dre."

"You know, she could have left him," Carrie said.

"Right." Hal laughed as he tied up the bag.

From the street they heard metallic wheezing. They looked out the window and saw an elderly garbage truck grinding slowly up the block, as if its wheels and gears could hardly bear its burden of trash. Hal grabbed two bags and ran down the icy front walk. Carrie waited until the door squealed behind him, then she wrapped Deidre's ceramic Bible in the daisy pillowcase and boxed it up for the basement. For a joke, she tucked Hal's 1990 *Britannica Year in Review* into the box. She wanted to see when he'd notice it was gone.

She herself could not remember much about 1990, outside of work, which had been devoted in large part to the Westminster Platinum Razor and Mother Goose Microwave Porky Pies. Steve and Deidre probably hadn't even met each other yet. Carrie was certain that she could imagine them: Steve smiling and pinkly shaven, a boy thrilled by fast cars, weekends, and his own pounding pulse; Deidre plump and blonde, a shopper, her heart pointed at the future. Sewing curtains, taking pregnancy tests, while Steve turned up the stereo volume, hungry for heat and laughter.

Carrie could hear Hal back at work in the library. She picked up a legal pad and walked around the boxes and upended tables in the living room, sketching possible furniture arrangements. How had they accumulated so much, living in apartments? Struggling with her floor plans, Carrie found herself irritated with Hal for spending the whole morning in the library when there was so much else to be done—the bed, for one thing. She crafted several withering remarks. But as she stood in the library doorway, penciling in extra shelves, Hal looked up from a slippery heap of magazines and said, "Our wedding was nice."

"Yes." She smiled at the page, marking Hal with an X. "I remember."

Actually, she'd met him in 1984. He was just starting out then, trying to stretch a master's in journalism over the bones of the real world, writing press releases for a company that made men's hygiene products. Carrie was a marketing intern learning how to walk in heels and talk to grown-ups; her company test-marketed the products that Hal's company created. Hal's CEO, a gregarious show-off, had thrown an Independence Day barbecue at his weekend house, and Carrie's boss Helen had invited her along.

It had been a dry summer, and the air reeked of exposed river mud. A boar with a missing ear revolved on a spit beside the pool. Everyone was talking about Reagan and restaurants. After a few gin and tonics, Carrie's feelings of intimidation gradually settled down to boredom. She wandered away from the conversations on the lawn, into the CEO's stone house. She had never been in a rich person's home before and almost giggled out loud when she came upon a library straight out of the movies, outfitted with leather chairs, drawn velvet curtains, and shelves of expensive-looking books. A reading stand was reverently lighted against the far wall, and a man stood before it, bowed priestlike over an open volume. Raw flaps of hair hung around his neck, and his white collar was dull and crushed from poor laundering.

Carrie stood in the doorway, shifting from foot to foot. Her new sandals stung. "That looks important," she said.

The young man gave his neck a nasty-looking wrench before he turned around. "You've got to see this," he said. He flipped back the cover of the lighted book on the altar: *The Encyclopedia of Classic American Cars*. And he and Carrie had grinned at each other and gone back to the party and danced to the hired band for an hour, even though Carrie's heels burned and Hal was a shy and anguished dancer.

Carrie could summon this memory with snapshot clarity but tended not to; sometimes it left her sore from rearview longing. Hal hadn't changed that much, physically, though his hair was quite a bit shorter now, as if winched irreversibly backward by the steady precision ticking of his brain. He now focused upon the larger issues of marketing. His grasp of the big picture was remarkable. Drawing upon little more than instinct and survey data, Hal could predict that media-driven working-class aspirations would sufficiently offset flat middle-class disposable income to assure a bright future for Spartacus hair care products and the Westminster Platinum Razor. On such matters, Carrie stood in awe of her husband.

He had always been more handsome from the back.

Saturday afternoon, Carrie sat on the flowered tiles of the bathroom floor, pulling cans and bottles from under the sink, marveling at the array of cleansers Deidre had left behind. So far, Carrie and Hal had moved the same can of furniture polish to three different addresses.

They were educated people, conversant about politics, wine, and dance, snobbish about vegetables and movies. But they were dirty. Laundry languished in the hamper. Their rooms were squalid with eviscerated newspapers, rusted fruit rinds, drifting clots of hair and dust. There was no reason to think that this house would be any different. Mess didn't much bother Hal, who often traveled on business, but Carrie sometimes felt bad about the way they lived. The chicken, for example, that she'd planned to make into curry—all week she'd been peeking at it, perched in its plastic on the top refrigerator shelf, but she couldn't make herself check to see if it had spoiled.

Carrie squirted a bit of Deidre's French Country Peach air freshener, just from curiosity, then reared back, flapping her hand to dispel the synthetic fruit and flowers. She instantly recognized the scent and the women who bought it.

Duckies. That's what Carrie's boss called them, those youngish wives who prided themselves on keeping things clean and spent more than they should on home decoration. They were especially fond of country-craftsy things, hence their nickname. They were an important and active segment of the female consumer market, but, according to Helen, in the next ten to fifteen years they would mutate into the Walking Wounded. Nests knocked awry, they would be on the market for eye creams, streamlining undergarments, college degrees, and men who didn't mind other men's children.

Carrie didn't bother showing the peach room spray to Hal.

They spent the rest of Saturday flattening boxes and throwing them down the basement stairs. On Sunday they tried arranging the living-room furniture and almost got into two arguments. By the end of the weekend, Carrie had managed to confiscate and hide all of Hal's yearbooks, except for 1989, which she could not bring herself to pack away, even as a joke.

They lived together three years before they decided to get married. Their friends' marriages were already starting to fail, and they were determined to avoid the usual pitfalls. There would be no diamond ring, no tossed bouquet, no fate-baiting vows of eternal love. Leery of both church and city hall, they invited their friends and family to an old fishing club upriver from the city. The lodge was chilly but cheap and spacious. Frail nets hung in swags from the rafters; the plank walls were decorated with antique rods and spears, and old faded life jackets. Carrie remembered swans on the river and her tight wedding shoes. Hal's father making his nervous toast—all Carrie could hear were the words "the threshold of life," repeated three times. Her mother sitting alone, delicately coughing on a fish bone. Silver heaps of gifts, clouds stretched across the moon.

There was a dam above the lodge, and when the siren sounded at midnight, warning that water was being released, the wedding guests rushed out to the wooden dock so they could feel the river rise under their feet. They kissed and hugged like New

Year's as the old dock creaked and bounced beneath them. Carrie's feet hurt so much that she kicked her shoes into the rushing current, and everyone except her mother applauded.

For years people had been telling Carrie what a wonderful wedding it had been. "The simplicity of that old lodge was very touching," Helen said. "It made me think that people could get married after all."

"We just couldn't afford any better," Carrie said.

"Maybe so, but it seemed to me you were walking the tightrope just right. And you have, haven't you? Speaking of which, we have a big group of Duckies coming in next week. Herbal fabric softener."

Helen was by her own admission a former member of the Walking Wounded. "What are you now?" Carrie once asked.

The older woman had laughed and patted Carrie's cheek. "Now? Now I don't buy shit. I don't mind helping others, though."

Three weeks into the new house, mornings were still difficult. The furnace ran hot; they awoke overheated and twisted up in their sleeping bags, crowded but alone, and raw from dreams. On Saturdays they were roused by the shrieking of the rusty garbage truck. Weekdays, they elbowed each other for space at the too-small bathroom mirror.

One Friday morning Carrie stood showered and naked before her open dresser drawer, hoping that a clean pair of panties would present themselves, when Hal came out of the bathroom toweling his wet hair with one hand and waving Deidre's can of French Country Peach air freshener with the other. "Look what I found."

Carrie waved him away, preoccupied with her search. She really had to buy new underwear. Stockings, too.

"You have to smell this to believe it," he said.

"I already did—no!" But it was too late. The can erupted. Hal and Carrie pulled back from each other, pinching their noses.

Hal began rifling his clothes pile, one hand pressed to his face. "It smells so pathetic," he said. "Where are my shirts?"

"Sorry, I didn't do laundry."

"It was your turn."

"I got home too late last night. Industrial peach." Carrie pulled on the bedraggled pink panties she wore only as a last resort. Her sinuses itched from the spray. "There are a lot of smells like that, where people recognize the chemical imitation and put a real name on it without even thinking. Rose, vanilla—" A worm of broken elastic danced on her thigh.

"I know," Hal snapped. "I read the same studies you do."

"What's the matter?"

"My cab's going to be here in fifteen minutes, and I'm still half naked."

Carrie had forgotten that he was flying to Houston that morning. But there it was, his black bag, poised by the bedroom door.

"I said I was sorry," she said, more sharply than she intended.

"You know what that spray smells like? Like they took every ridiculous idea that wom—" quickly, Hal corrected himself—"that decent Americans ever had about romance, and they mixed it up with some candy hearts and Hallmark cards and supermarket roses and feminine hygiene spray"—he was rolling now, tuning his contempt like a guitar—"and you boiled it all together in a crummy old factory somewhere in Milwaukee or Detroit, and this is what you came up with."

"I didn't come up with it."

"Let's face it, you would have helped them sell it if they'd hired you. To poor little critters like what's-her-name—"

"Deidre."

"What?" He sniffed the armpit of an eighty-dollar shirt, tossed it aside.

"That's her name, Deidre."

"Deidre. Of course." He grinned at Carrie as she wrestled with her too-tight gabardine skirt. When she refused to smile back, he walked across the room and squirted peach spray onto her arm.

"You're as guilty as I am," Carrie said. She walked into the bathroom, locked the door, and shakily sat on the edge of the sarcophagus-size Jacuzzi. She was breathless—frightened by her own rage and sickened by the smell on her skin. She rubbed her arm with a washcloth, to no avail. In addition to Hal's inventory of pathetic ingredients, she could detect traces of baby wipes and lavender. Poor Deidre. Carrie stripped off her clothes and climbed back into the shower, just as Hal shyly knocked on the other side of the door.

"Carrie? I'm sorry. I know that stuff smells bad. If anyone at work mentions it, just tell them that I love it. All right? Blame me."

"OK." She pressed her forehead against the shower tiles.

"You're right, I'm guilty too. But my cab's here." Through the closed door she could hear him struggling with the sleeves of his jacket. "I'll be back Monday. All right?"

"I'm ovulating," she said, but she didn't unlock the door. In any case, he'd already run down the hall.

After her shower, Carrie threw the peach spray into the bathroom trash. She emptied the bathroom trash into the kitchen trash, took a deep breath, pulled the chicken out of the refrigerator, and threw that away too. As she closed the bag, she tried not to look at the grisly contents. How stupid they had been to buy clear garbage bags. Clear plastic had seemed honest and somehow better than white—or pink—but Carrie now realized that she could not stand the sight of what they threw away.

She marched the bag out to the can by the garage. After work she went to the mall and bought suede shoes, a beige summer suit, and one hundred and eighty dollars worth of underwear and stockings.

That evening she alternately hated and missed Hal. The anger didn't surprise her; she'd felt it before, plenty of times. But in the city she used to like being alone for a few days, free to do as she pleased. In this house, surrounded by bare walls, she felt forsaken. She reminded herself that in another few hours her hormones would settle down. She reminded herself that she didn't want children, only her body did; she and Hal had decided to let nature take its course, and nature had made its decision. At bedtime she could not face the sleeping bags. She pulled out Hal's old plaid sheets and her mother's unraveling afghan and slept on the living-room sofa—tried to, anyway, until she got tangled up remembering.

August 1984. Her first night at Hal's apartment. Midnight. He had stalled for a long time, playing jazz records, reading aloud from his master's thesis, pushing his shirtsleeves up and down. Finally, she'd just pulled open the sofa bed and stretched out in her rayon suit on the brown plaid sheets. She'd had to help him with the floppy bow on her blouse, and other things, and his clumsiness had touched and excited her. That night Carrie's love was like a too-hot platter she had to set down, but she knew that she shouldn't say "I love you," not out loud, not yet. So she stroked the back of his head and said, "I love the way you talk. You're supercilious." She thought it meant something like "superior." And Hal had laughed and hugged her, trembling and hot, just as she was, and clung to her for a long time, pulling back only for a moment, to crack his neck.

How proud she had been of herself, for years, for navigating the reefs that night. Deidre, she was certain, would have blurted out "I love you" and suffered the consequences.

Now Deidre was alone, and Hal and Carrie were still together. Carrie considered these results from many angles before she finally fell asleep.

She woke up early Saturday morning but despite her best intentions could not face the disordered house alone. She put on her new linen suit and suede shoes, just to try them. She was practicing walking on the slippery soles when the doorbell rang.

The decrepit garbage truck was muttering at the curb, and a uniformed middle-aged woman stood on the front step, holding one of the clear garbage bags. "Ma'am, I can't take this." Through the plastic Carrie could see the chicken, lounging on a nest of bathroom trash. "The county says I can't take aerosol cans." The woman pointed to Deidre's room spray, which was flanked by tampon tubes and a greasy pizza box.

"But it's not mine," Carrie said. "The woman who lived here before, she left it behind." The January air soaked her thin suit; she hugged herself.

The woman smiled and set the sack at Carrie's feet. "Take it out, please."

Children across the street had been swashbuckling with icicles. Now they suspended their battle to stare. Carrie knelt on the threshold and untwisted the tie, loosing a stench of wasted food. She pushed up the sleeve of her jacket and reached inside, picking through chow mein noodles, egg shells, and wet snarls of hair, holding up her sleeve with one hand, breathing through her mouth. Hal had thrown away a full carton of sour milk, which had spattered everything. The children whispered and giggled. Her bangs were sticking to her forehead. As she pulled out the slimy can of room spray, a tea bag fell on her shoe.

"What am I supposed to do with it?" she asked.

She crouched on the threshold of her house, shivering, stretching out helpless, soiled hands. The woman pulled a rag from her pocket and wiped Carrie's palms, then her cheeks, pushing her hair out of her eyes. "It's not that bad," she said, helping Carrie to her feet.

Carrie pulled down her damp sleeve. Determined to salvage some dignity, she said, in her focus-group voice, "Would you say we have an average amount of trash or more than average?"

The woman smiled patiently. "It doesn't matter, you pay the same whatever."

"Did you know the people before us? With the pink bags?"

"Just worry about what you throw out, that's what I tell everybody. You'd better take care of that shoe or it'll stain." She picked up Carrie's sack, walked to the curb, and tossed it into the rear of the truck.

Carrie went inside and kicked off the shoes. She ran hot water over her chilled hands. She rinsed the can of room spray, dried it, and walked around the house for a while holding it in the crook of her arm. Then she went downstairs.

The unfinished basement was poorly lighted and crowded

with the boxes Carrie and Hal had no plans to open: the tacky old things, the never-wanted things. The box with Deidre's ceramic wedding Bible and the hidden *Britannica* annuals was right where Carrie had left it. She pulled the little shrine out of the daisy pillowcase and set it on a high shelf, next to the pink trash bags. She set the room spray beside it. Then she unpacked the eleven yearbooks she'd hidden and carried them back upstairs. It took two trips.

Carrie was astonished to see that Hal had left the 1989 volume spread open on the library carpet. Heedless of her new suit, she sat on the floor and gathered the heavy book onto her lap.

They'd written their own wedding service. She could no longer remember exactly what they had promised one another. Nothing outlandish, she was certain of that. While Hal spoke his vows, Carrie's eyes had slipped from his nervous face to the old life jackets hanging on the wall behind him. She wondered if they could still save anyone. Just before the judge proclaimed them married, Carrie reached over and pulled a straight pin from the collar of Hal's new shirt.

"Your pretty shoes," her mother had cried, after her white sandals floated downstream. "Why?"

"Just taking the curse off." She'd been a little drunk and very happy.

She gave her wedding dress to her cousin, but she'd kept the pin, stuck in a bar of soap from their hotel suite.

They hadn't wanted to need each other too much. They had done their best to avoid it, but it had happened anyway.

Suddenly, Carrie wanted to find the pin. She knew it was somewhere in the bedroom, maybe with the jewelry boxes and scarves she'd dumped on the closet floor. But once she was in the bedroom, she saw the box springs leaning against the wall, and she forgot about the pin. She decided to put the bed together herself.

When she hauled the sleeping bags off the mattress, she found that they'd been zipped together into one big bag. Hal must have done it just before he left for Houston.

The queen-size mattress was floppy, ungainly; the box springs slipped and dropped on her bare foot, bruising the toenails. Still, she managed to put it all together. She covered the mattress with the plaid sheets and spread the coupled sleeping bags over everything. Just as she finished, Hal called.

He told her about the Houston dampness and the demographic conference and the prospects for a new line of men's facial masks. He asked her if she still hated him.

She leaned back on the mattress, which seemed precariously high after its weeks on the floor. "Off and on. You know. Hormones."

"I know." He let the conversation rest for a moment. Then, "I'm wrapping up early here and flying out in a few hours. I'll be back about midnight."

"Good. I miss you."

"When you aren't hating me."

"I can do both at the same time. Can't you?"

He laughed. "The long haul."

Carrie thought she could smell sour milk on the sleeve of her new jacket. At least her body had settled down, dropping the subject for another month. She debated telling Hal about the garbage lady and the peach spray, but decided to save it for later, when they were together in the dark. Then they would laugh—about what? Maybe about all the things they had not been able to avoid. She said, "I like the sleeping bags—bag, I should say."

"We can put the bed together tomorrow."

"I already did, just now."

"But it's so heavy."

"I smashed my foot. Monday morning, I won't be able to get my shoe on."

"Hang on." He set the phone down. She heard him crack his neck and smiled—she could practically feel the bones fall into their proper place.

After they said good-bye, Carrie stretched out across the sleeping bag. She decided to take a nap, suit and all. She shouldn't. There was so much to do around the house. But she had plenty of time.

I Love You, Spartacus

The movie is starting, but Alice has lost her husband. In search of his favorite theater seats, twelfth row center, Ben rushed ahead into the blackness, leaving Alice blind and stranded in the aisle with nothing to guide her except a strip of lights as tiny and unhelpful as the stars. Usually, he tows her behind him, but today he's too excited to remember.

Self-consciously she crouches, knowing how she hates it when people are still stumbling around after the movie has started. How large and stupid she feels! She can't see anything except the bright, unfurling credits. In her confusion she's about to grope backward to the lobby, when suddenly her eyes adjust, and she sees Ben's white cashmere arm waving to her through the darkness. She bends over and scurries to the seat beside his.

"You're a hard gal to ditch," Ben whispers, beneath the blare of soundtrack trumpets. Alice kisses his ear and hands him the bottle of mineral water she smuggled in under her coat. She counts back rows: twelve.

This is a special day for Alice and Ben. It's the local premiere of *Spartacus*, the restored version with the suggestive bath scene between Laurence Olivier and Tony Curtis. That's not why they came. Alice and Ben are here because they are fans of the Hollywood historical epic. Anything with Romans or Biblical heroes—they like the sequins, the Man Tan, the cheery falseness of it all. Nobody is fooling anybody, and it's fine. Usually, they must content themselves with rented videotapes, but today *Spartacus* is lavishly spread before them, on the last wide screen in the city, and they can sink into the splendor happy that this time, at least, they're smaller than the epic.

Ben and Alice have been married for eleven months. It's been a marriage of movies. They consecrate their passion every Sunday:

Ben, who always wakes up first, retrieves the newspaper from the hall, puts on his robe, climbs back into bed, and spreads the theater listings across the quilt. The quilt was a wedding present; once white, it is now lightly shadowed with ink. But the movie is the main thing. Huddled together over the paper, Ben and Alice sometimes will debate for an hour before making their choice.

Alice and Ben couldn't wait until Sunday to see *Spartacus*. Ben took off early from his job at the library, and Alice put off looking for work one more day, so they could attend this first showing, at four o'clock on a Friday afternoon.

Despite how much Alice has looked forward to *Spartacus*, the movie does not disappoint. Not only does it have all the elements of a fine epic—decadent Romans, virtuous slave girls, sneaky Turks—but it's actually a quality movie. While the slaves endure their abuse, Alice smiles at Ben, tenderly, in the reflected light from the screen. She hunts for his hand on his lap. When Spartacus inspires the gladiators to revolt, Alice lays her head on Ben's shoulder, moved by something sharper than love, moved by gratitude for her own fine luck.

Only a year and a half ago, she was waiting tables at a tourist steakhouse. Her calves ached in the mornings; she ground her teeth at night. She was twenty-nine years old, her roommates left hairs in the shower, and no man was even close to being right. It wasn't as if she was holding out for a Moses or a Samson. No, Alice was willing to settle for less—Basil Rathbone, say, mixed with choice bits of Ralph Nader and Jacques Pepin. But all she ever got were men with linty berets, soy breath, and a tendency, while standing in movie lines, to loudly use words like "pretentious" and "sentimental." Men who claimed solidarity with the oppressed but never would take her word that she didn't have a G spot.

One night she went to a Hitchcock festival with a forty-year-old graduate student named Eric. He was carrying a knapsack which that evening contained an especially pungent piece of cheese. They were standing in the theater lobby after *Shadow of a Doubt*, and Eric was shredding the film with gerbilish zeal. He was so intent upon impressing Alice that he didn't notice she wasn't listening at all; she was looking at the man behind him, a younger man who at each of Eric's pronouncements would smile at her and tear with mock desperation at the throat of his handsome sweater. After *Suspicion*, in the snack line, she found herself standing next to the young man. She noted his sharp blue eyes and the noble slant of his nose. He dropped a lemon peel into her paper cup of espresso, glanced back toward Eric, and said, "Have you noticed that nobody uses the word 'egomaniac' anymore?" By the time *Vertigo* began, Alice and Ben were sitting in a cafe far away, drinking Kona coffee and trading their favorite lines from *The Ten Commandments*.

Sometimes she tells Ben that she married him simply because he didn't own a beret. He claims he married her because one of her girlfriends slept with the prince of epics, Victor Mature.

Alice enjoys being married to Ben. Like *Spartacus*, he has exceeded her expectations. He leaves funny notes on her pillow, gives her warm socks and thick sweaters. "It's November," he says, "cover up, cover up." When she lost her job at the restaurant, he told her not to worry. When she put off looking for new work, he didn't care. Things have always been a bit slight on the bedroom side, but this doesn't matter much to Alice, who has long suspected that the rest of the world exaggerates its sex life. Anyway, she reminds herself, you can't have everything.

Ben is a master of concentration. It's a hobby of his. He can read a novel in an ATM line; he can catnap sitting up in a subway car. He watches movies in a trance, never speaking, barely breathing. But today is different. Ben seems a little jumpy. He snickers when the famous bath scene begins. When they start talking about oysters and snails, he actually snorts. When the love theme plays, he makes faint gagging sounds. Alice is perplexed. True, the music is insipid, and Kirk Douglas and Jean Simmons look awfully posh for runaway slaves, but isn't that what she and Ben have always loved about these movies?

She doesn't really mind this mood of his, she's just surprised. She reminds herself that she hasn't known him for very long. Maybe she has a lot more to learn.

She remembers how surprised she was when she found out about the projections. That's what he called the occasional trips he took without her—after the wedding, for example, when they were driving down the California coast. Coming into Big Sur, Ben said, "I'm off to India now," and just like that he was beholding the cremation ghats and holy Ganges. He told her about it later. He's also gone to Iceland, Morocco, and the Yucatán. Once he asked her, "You don't mind, do you?" "Not as long as you come back," she said.

During the intermission Alice sits, slightly stunned, on a naugahyde lobby bench, surrounded by the lower halves of her fellow moviegoers. She notes that while a black-and-white movie makes the real world look as garish as plaid pants, a color movie like *Spartacus* shows real life for the murky aquarium it is. The crowd consists of gay men, aging military types, Eric-style film students, and blinky old ladies, probably there for the same love music that makes Ben gag. He's in the snack line, buying drinks; she can't see him because a man's denim behind is in her face. To avoid it, she looks out the lobby window to the sidewalk. It's dark November out there, and people are on their way home from work. Rain needles their shoulders and feet. Despite this, they march on, their arms filled with grocery bags, bakery boxes, drooping bunches of flowers. She admires them, but still, she's glad she's at the movies.

Alice and Ben met here, in this lobby. Just looking at the blistered mauve walls makes her remember the cheese smell of Eric's knapsack and the hopeful sight of Ben's white sweater.

That night Alice and Ben said the sort of things you can only say the first time you talk to someone.

Alice said, "I'm tired of always waiting for somebody who's not wrong."

Ben said, "I'm tired of people always expecting things of me."

"Women, you mean?"

He nodded, made a face. "But I'll be thirty next year. I'd better make up my mind."

They began having dinners and, of course, going to movies. One night, after *Ben-Hur*, they came back to Ben's flat, and while he dripped coffee, Alice made a fire and found a typed list atop the kindling. *1. Movies. 2. V. Mature story. 3. Congenial undemanding natures. 4. Our genteel desperation.*

"What's this?" she said.

He leaned out of the kitchen, just the top half of him, beating a bowl of cream. "Reasons we should join our mighty empires."

"You want to live together?"

"No." The whisk scraped against the stainless steel bowl.

"You mean get married?" The last word shyly stumbled on her tongue. They'd slept together three times, once in T-shirts.

Ben laughed. "Duh, Alice," he said, and he pulled back into the kitchen. He raised his voice over a clatter of dishes. "People do it for stupider reasons."

"I know."

"What?" A spoon skidded across the floor.

"Yes!"

Alice's roommates thought she was crazy to marry someone she'd never even fought with, but she was proud of herself and Ben for tying up their loose futures with so little fuss. *Congenial undemanding natures*. The description seemed cozy and wise. Safe, even.

She watches him wind toward her through the crowd, balancing her hot cup in one hand, his cold one in the other. He never spills. He doesn't drink coffee anymore. Sometime last summer he began shifting to mineral water. Now that's all he drinks. Alice finds the bottles everywhere—drained on the nightstand, clanking on the floor of the car. Meanwhile, she's more addicted to caffeine than ever. Sometimes she wakes up at three in the morning with her nerves flashing like sparklers and her brain full of stupid questions like, "Have I already had the best day of my life?"

Ben hands her the coffee, just as the intermission bell rings. "I forgot to tell you. Sammy's meeting us for dinner."

Alice tries to look pleased. Sammy is Ben's best friend and former fraternity brother. Ben maintains that Sammy is secretly gay, something to do with his lips and the way he presses his knees together when he's standing in line. These clues fly straight over Alice's head, though she does find them amusing. Anyway, it's not Sammy's sexual orientation that bothers her. It's not really anything he does; he's always friendly and polite. But Sammy always makes Alice feel like a bully, as if she's loudly demanding things, insisting upon things, even as she says nothing at all. Which is ridiculous. She's very shy with him.

The audience files back into the theater, and a big battle sets up. Roman legions move in clanking formation, then, seemingly from nowhere, a thousand armed slaves rush forward to claim their freedom. Horses rear, swords clash, a wheel of fire mows down a line of Romans—and the slaves lose. Alice is surprised, but she assumes that a bigger battle is forthcoming.

After the slaves' defeat, comrades Tony Curtis and Kirk Douglas are forced by cruel Olivier to fight each other to the death. But instead of killing Kirk, Tony embraces him and says, "I love you, Spartacus." At this, Ben laughs out loud. An old lady hisses him. He tries to stop, but the laughter keeps coming, in harsh gasps. Unable to laugh with Ben—she's not sure what's so funny—Alice can only pat his arm and shush him, as Tony Curtis valiantly lets himself be killed.

Slowly, Ben manages to quiet down, watching the screen from under his hand. Alice settles back in anticipation of the battle that will free the slaves and end the movie.

But they crucify Spartacus! Alice can't believe it—at any moment she expects him to jump down from the cross and sprint to freedom. Instead, he just hangs there with all the other dying rebels, and Jean Simmons drives off with homely Peter Ustinov. Why? What could the filmmakers have been thinking? Alice looks to Ben, but he's once again submerged in the movie. She reminds herself that this is a Stanley Kubrick film. Still, it's most unsatisfying. She means to ask Ben about it when they leave, but she doesn't really have a chance; he's hustling her through the rain to the restaurant where they will meet Sammy.

The Hurricane is an old Polynesian restaurant that has bamboo furniture, Tiki masks, passable food, and a framed gallery of long-ago celebrity customers. The innocence of this decor appeals to Alice and Ben the same way epic movies do. Whenever they come here, Ben makes Alice tell the story of her girlfriend and Victor Mature, whose large, somewhat confused-looking face is among those mounted on the wall.

This evening Alice orders a Moby Dick cocktail. She wants Ben to try a Captain Bligh, but he insists upon mineral water.

He buries himself in his menu even though he always gets the same thing, stir-fried vegetables. There's a musty draft in the air. The candle on their table sputters and smokes. A few feet away a bucket is catching drips from a blackened corner of the fake-grass ceiling. There are no other customers.

Alice says, "I'm upset about Spartacus."

Ben glances up from his menu, a bit sharply.

She says, "I assumed he'd get away at the end."

He looks back down. "Impossible."

"What do you mean, he was real?"

"Duh, Alice."

"Well." Blushing, she examines her own menu. History isn't her subject. Only last year did she learn that Confucius was not a made-up legend, like Frankenstein.

She says, "Why did you laugh so hard at poor Tony Curtis?"

Ben dips his face and plucks a hair, one of hers, from his sleeve. "Didn't you notice? It was the climax of the whole gay theme."

Alice hadn't noticed, but, still smarting from her historical blunder, she decides not to say so. "I just don't see why it was funny."

"Because." He fries the hair over the candle flame, waves away the smell. "They thought they were putting one over on us innocent movie fans, back then. Not today, though." He pushes up his sleeves. "Where's Sammy, I wonder?"

Alice's Moby Dick turns out to be a snifter of frothy blue acid. She pushes it aside, orders an espresso, and for the first time in her marriage, she wishes that Sammy was there.

Why is she so vexed? She rules out the rain, the drafty restaurant, Ben's behavior at the movie. Right now he seems to be projecting himself someplace; she doesn't ask where. Manhattan, Madagascar—what difference does it make, really? She's here.

Finally, Sammy arrives, drenched and sniffling. He unwinds a long scarf from his throat. "How was the movie? Hello, Alice."

"Majestic," Ben says. "Awe-inspiring."

"Except for the ending," Alice says.

"Spartacus died," Ben says. "Alice had gotten kind of attached to him."

Sammy says, "Spartacus was hung up next to Jesus, right?"

Ben mimes shooting himself in the ear. "I give up."

Sammy stands beside the booth for a moment, hesitating, then chooses Alice's side. He scans the menu. "They have Kumamoto oysters."

Ben grins at Alice. "I'd rather have snails. No, cancel that. I want oysters *and* snails." He bursts out in another metallic laugh, as if he's coughing up a ball of rusty wire. Sammy looks baffled but says nothing.

Alice decides that even if Sammy has gay inclinations, he can't possibly have a sex life. For one thing, he's too dumpy, at least compared to most of the gay men she sees, in the ads for health clubs and 900 numbers. Those men have heroic jaws and torsos, whereas Sammy has only his earnestness to recommend him. And it's an earnestness that borders on stupidity. Last Christmas he sent out a computer letter telling everyone about his adult acne and recent Barium enema.

To atone for these peevish thoughts, Alice offers to split some oysters with Sammy.

Ben is still holding forth on *Spartacus*. Sometimes Alice gets irritated by the slavish attention Sammy pays to Ben, but now she realizes that it's no different from her own. The fact is, Ben is fun, for one simple reason: He enjoys being himself. Right now, for example, rehashing the Roman Empire, kind of harping on the historical part of it.

And she realizes, that's it, that's the problem: Spartacus, the man. She's not mad at him; he did the best he could. She's mad at Hollywood for not making up someone better. As it was, there was never the possibility of a good ending, and Alice feels cheated. Worse, she feels like a chump.

She wants to ask Ben why Hollywood didn't do better by Spartacus, but their dinner arrives and she's distracted by the oysters, which she doesn't even like. Then Ben switches subjects, from *Spartacus* to *Rain* and its corny but effective use of native drums to build sexual tension. Sammy's and Alice's eyes are starting to glaze when a young man in denim walks into the restaurant and sits at the bar. Blond and bright-faced, younger than all of them, he shakes off the rain with puppy impatience and refuses to order a drink. It seems that he's waiting for someone. Back and forth he twists on the revolving bar stool, scornfully appraising the old Tiki heads. He's so fresh, so arrogant—they can't stop looking at him.

Alice is the first to turn away; she wants to see Sammy's reaction to this vision. But Sammy isn't looking at the boy, he's looking at Ben with something like alarm. Ben doesn't notice, he's caught up in staring at the boy. Alice keeps expecting him to break off and say something funny, but he doesn't, he just keeps watching, with no expression at all.

Sammy glances from Ben to Alice. She smiles and shrugs. It's OK, she wants to tell him, I don't mind. As the three of them sit there, watching the boy and listening to the ceiling drip, Alice's unspoken assurance takes on color and nerve and begins dancing behind her eyes, mincing this way and that in a frothy pink skirt. *It's OK, I don't mind* . . . over and over, in an insipid Shirley Temple voice. Alice sips her watery Moby Dick and tries to smile—she knows she's being ridiculous—but the world is suddenly heavy and cold, and for the second time that day she's lost in the dark, patting empty air with timid hands.

An older man with thin, wet hair walks in and greets the boy, who immediately demands to be taken to a place with people.

Ben turns away, pushing down his sweater sleeves. He sighs, picks up his half-eaten dinner, and sets it on the neighboring table. "Alice," he says, "have you told Sammy your Victor Mature story?"

"Who's Victor Mature?" Sammy says.

"Tell it, Alice."

For a moment, Alice looks blankly at Ben. She finally says, "It's just a plain old pick-up story."

Ben says, "Go on."

Though Alice has told Ben this story half a dozen times, suddenly it pains her to think of the elderly Victor Mature hanging around a hotel bar, drunk and hopeful that someone will want to go to bed with him. It pains her that she's embarrassed by these only-human urges on his part, and that they make her husband laugh.

She says, "I don't want to tell it anymore. I'm sure my friend made the whole thing up."

"Now you tell me." Ben looks to Sammy. "That's why I married her, you know, because she had this story."

"Honestly, Ben!" Sammy slaps the tabletop in exasperation. "That's not funny."

Alice stares at Sammy's round, worried face. He's really innocent. What will the world end up doing with him? She reaches over and touches one of his empty oyster shells. "It's OK," she says.

"Good grief." Ben lays some money on the table. He stands up. "Let's get out of here, you're both a couple of sticks tonight."

Neither Alice nor Sammy argues with him.

They pause by the photo gallery to put on their coats. Ben scans the wall of ancient faces. Chortling, he points to a framed glossy of Tony Curtis, just southwest of Victor Mature.

Sammy looks puzzled and slightly hurt. "I guess I should go to more movies."

"Aw, Sam." Ben hooks an arm around Sammy's plump neck. "Hey. I love you, Spartacus."

Sammy shoves Ben aside, grimaces at Alice. "OK. Sure."

She pats Sammy's arm. "Me too," she says, but in truth she's glad to be going home.

As they sit in the parking lot, waiting for the car to warm up, Ben says, "Why wouldn't you tell the Victor Mature story?"

Alice watches the old man from the bar hurry through the rain to his car. The bored boy is waiting for him under the fake-grass restaurant awning. She says, "Why shouldn't he have wanted someone that night?"

Ben doesn't answer. He's watching the boy, too.

For the first time, the ink-stained bed quilt depresses Alice, unreasonably, since she could easily take it to the cleaners. It's just that the quilt is so new. She climbs into bed and tries to think of something else. She doesn't usually have moods. Neither does Ben; it's one reason they get along so well. She lies between the chill sheets and waits for him to come out of the bathroom, where he's washing his face and putting on his pajamas.

The pajamas arrived with the winter rains. He was cold, he said. Each night he would emerge from the bathroom buttoned up in yards of flannel. The first few nights it was nice to press up against all that toasty cloth, then Alice started feeling too naked. She bought a pair of her own pajamas, in a matching plaid, and now she and Ben sleep side by side like a couple of friendly lumberjacks.

He slides under the covers, and she rolls up against him, demanding warmth. Briskly, he rubs her back. He yawns. She lays an inquiring finger upon his hip. He leans over and kisses her on the chin. "I love you, Spartacus," he says. He yawns again, so hard he shudders, and turns onto his stomach.

There's a streetlight outside their second-story window. It casts a ragged screen of orange on the wall. Alice says, "Why?"

"Why what?"

"Why do you love me?"

She knows what he wants to say. *I was kidding, Alice, duh.* But of course he can't say that.

"You're kind," he says. "You have a good sense of humor."

"God. Don't tell me I have a nice personality."

He reaches over and taps her on the skull. "Not at all. In fact, you're very nice-looking. And you're very nice to me." With this, he rolls onto his side and, it seems, instantly falls asleep.

Alice isn't upset with him, only with herself. She didn't even want sex, she just wanted to lay claim. How awful. Isn't that why they married each other, because they were beyond all that? How she hates having moods—it must be all the coffee she drank at dinner. Her body is a horse spooked and ready to run, dragging her frightened brain behind it. If she were Ben, she would project herself right now to a suitable place, a rodeo or a boxing ring. But since she's not Ben, she can only fix her eyes on the screen of light on the wall and let the pictures come: the rampaging slaves; Ben hiding his face and laughing at Tony Curtis; the Hurricane with its drip bucket and platters of oysters; Spartacus, hanging; Ben watching the boy at the bar, his face a careful lid on what he's thinking—

It's OK, I don't mind.

Alice stops the projector behind her eyes, listens to the reverberating plea.

Should she mind?

No!

Really, why should she? Ben made his choice. At worst, he only wants to, and what does that matter, really? Is it any different from going to India without her?

Anyway, it's a stupid thing to worry about. Caffeine and hormones, that's all it is. She should switch to water, too. She should be more like Ben, disciplined and well-informed. She turns over and looks at him, all covered up except for a handful of hair. She touches his warm head. Nothing is different.

Again she remembers their wedding trip. They drove down the coast, stopping one day, at her insistence, to walk through a grove of giant redwoods. Raindrops were falling from far above; Alice tried to catch them in her mouth. She felt dwarfed and mortal beside the ancient trees, but happy to be alive and married to someone so right, so organized and clever. But Ben wasn't enjoying it; he was trudging behind her, silent, his head down. "Redwood stumps last five hundred years," she said, to cheer him up and also to show off a little, but he just stared at her, and she had a premonition that he was about to tell her something bad. So when he sat her down on a rain-soaked stump, put his hands on her face and said, "I hate it here, it's just too much," she laughed in relief and kissed his eyes. They went back to the city that night and stayed in an expensive hotel suite with thick bathrobes and two big beds.

She used to wonder why Ben, so comfortable with history, could not face those factual trees. Now she feels the same aversion, and anger, too: at a world that refused to let you be, that insisted upon logic and conclusions, gravity, bright light in your eyes, when you'd been happy enough on the dim edge of things.

Alice holds fast to Ben's slack, sleeping hand. Before her the grass ceiling drips, drips, drips. The Tiki masks glower and tilt. The boy at the bar keeps twirling, spinning himself into a blur, a funnel, a tornado that roars across the city—

No, it's just Ben, snoring. Alice listens to her husband. His snores don't go back and forth like most people's, they have a relentless forward quality to them, like a saw—she can see it, a circular blade as tall as a movie screen, chewing through that redwood forest, leaving nothing but raw stumps and a mountain of chips. Ben is marching up the side of the sloppy heap. How well he keeps his balance! At the summit he turns and waves to her. She calls to him, she tries to follow him, but the mountain is moving, shuddering, pulling itself upward, and she's tossed down to the floor of the wrecked forest, where nothing remains but Ben's discarded white sweater.

Ben's gone, but before Alice can mourn, Spartacus rises healed before her. Beneath a sky of scalded blue he stands, victorious, waving his drenched sword. Rome lies shattered behind him; all enemies have fled his rage and might. He's looking dead ahead. Alice can't see what he sees, but she knows: He's arrived at the place where he belongs.

Careful

When Patty sees Garrett in his new swim trunks, her heart springs up like a cobra.

It's not just his extreme thinness and whiteness, as if he's been somebody's prisoner. It's also the scars. Though not large, they are plentiful, scattered across his back and chest and legs, some pale and reserved, others rosy with youth. After a year of marriage, Patty has accepted the scars, but she never ceases to notice them. Now, faced with an afternoon pool party at Garrett's parents' house, she's worried—what will the other guests think when they see the mortified flesh of her husband?

The swim trunks are wide, plaid, ridiculous. Garrett does a Paris runway strut across the living room, tossing his tangled black hair. She considers the striped shadows of his ribs.

"Maybe you should put on jeans and long sleeves," she says. "So you don't burn." Already at ten in the morning the July sun is clanging outside their apartment windows. Everything they own—her computer, his guitars, their herniated couch—looks sickly and dim inside the shades that Patty's pulled.

She says, "Maybe we should stay here."

"I thought you wanted to visit them." Garrett rarely says "parents," never "mother" or "father." He says, "Come on. It'll be, mmm, interesting."

Patty pushes his hair out of his eyes. "We could go downtown, instead."

He brushes her hand away from his face, then catches it and squeezes. "Patty. Say yes." This is something they told him in drug treatment, six months before she met him: Never say no if you can say yes. To life, that is. He accepted the advice as a jewel of wisdom and each day turns it this way and that, forcing Patty to admire it with him.

143

"Say it." He plants a line of joking kisses up her arm. She knows she should say, No, it won't be good for you, but he's so eager to jump into the day that for the hundredth time since that first nuptial yes, she surrenders.

The fact is, Patty hates Garrett's parents and has always wanted to meet them.

Until she married Garrett, Patty never thought of herself as a passionate person. She'd had a couple of affairs and a couple of jobs, she ate no red meat and watched no TV, she dreamed nothing worth repeating. Now sometimes she almost laughs when she sees her reflection: This plump computer programmer with dental braces and sensible shoes nourishes a hate so strong it can make her ears ring. It's a rocket ride hate, an atom bomb hate, and it's aimed directly at Garrett's parents, Bart and Martha Sunday.

They're throwing the pool party to celebrate the house they've just bought. The expensively printed invitation rattled Patty. She'd been a long time constructing a logical childhood for Garrett, and it depended in part on poverty. She realizes that she's probably used too many stock props like hot irons and dark closets, but she needs something to explain how a child could grow up to walk through three separate plates of glass, fall out of two apartment windows, crack his skull on tree branches and cupboard doors, and always grab the sharp side of the carving knife. All accidentally, he says. True, he was on drugs when most of this happened, but Patty believes in thoroughly codified laws of cause and effect. She thinks his parents hurt him.

The Sundays live an hour away, in the city's swankest, farthest suburb. Garrett called them last Christmas, but he didn't let Patty talk. As far as she knows, he never sees them. "They don't like me, I'm their worst memory," he said, laughing. He never mentions his childhood. When Patty brings it up, he says, "I love them." When she persists, he covers his ears and chants, "I love them, I love them, I do, I do," until she throws up her hands and shuts herself in the bedroom. Then he follows her in, and they take each other's clothes off.

∞

Patty's father drives a bus, but he's worth a quarter-million dollars in insurance. He believes in flu shots and family fire drills, and he has left his daughter with cautious habits and an immigrant's awe of the suburbs. She grew up in a Philadelphia apartment that seemed to darken and shrink with each passing year. She's way over her head at the Sundays' house.

The house is all glass. That's what Patty sees, anyway, when she and Garrett drive up—floor-to-ceiling windows, no curtains or shades. Patty and Garrett stand in the shrubbery and peer into the living room, where everything is modern and pale except for a bowl of cherries on the coffee table and a painting of something dark and abstract.

"What nerve," Patty says, trying to sound admiring.

Garrett doesn't answer. On the ride over he was full of jokes and old songs, but suddenly his hair is thrown forward over most of his face and he's wearing a pair of black sunglasses. His knees twang back and forth as he presses the doorbell. When no one comes to the door, he pushes it open as if expecting an ambush.

She wants to ask, Why are we here? Her protectiveness is at war with her curiosity; she's so thrilled and angry that she can barely breathe.

Ungreeted, Garrett and Patty wander through the big house, over yards of costly carpet, down a long hall, through a sun-blasted dining room and kitchen, to an outdoor patio filled with party guests. A black-tiled swimming pool flashes and hums in the center of the gathering. From here Patty sees that the house isn't all glass; there's a low second story decently covered with shingles.

Patty and Garrett live on the rear third floor of their building. It's a crowded neighborhood. At night the open windows let in the sounds of motorcycles, arias, domestic strife. Some evenings they just sit there and listen to their neighbors' wide-open lives, though Patty always enjoys the show more than Garrett does.

Now, at the edge of his parents' patio, Garrett digs at a scratch on his elbow, cranes his neck. "I don't see them. And I don't recognize anybody, they must have all new friends," he says, without irony.

The other guests are older—tanned white people with chipper clothing and well-toned smiles. No one is swimming. Everyone is trying not to stare at Garrett's long hair and lurid swim trunks. Patty, who always means to buy casual clothes, is wearing one of her work blouses and a pair of Garrett's shorts that are too tight and, she now realizes, have a smiling skull embroidered on the back pocket.

A man approaches them, lazily tilting his drink as if he doesn't care whether it spills. He says to Garrett, "And you are?"

"Hi." Garrett clears his throat, extends his hand. "Garrett. Sunday."

"Come again?"

"Bart," Garrett mutters. "Junior."

The man lifts Garrett's sunglasses and peers at him as if inspecting an exotic creature in a cage. He vigorously nods. "Yes, it's obvious. Uncanny, even. I'm afraid we've lost them."

"What?" Patty says.

"This is my wife," Garrett says. "Patty."

"I mean, we haven't seen your parents yet. I suppose they must have stepped out."

The man presents Garrett and Patty to his wife, who waves a freckled arm at the glass walls. "This is quite a house, isn't it?" she says. "The original family was blind! Don't you think it's marvelous to have such a sense of humor? But of course you knew that."

And so forth. For the next hour Garrett and Patty find themselves handed off from one guest to another, batons in a relay race of suburban curiosity. They answer questions, eat party meat, squint in the glaring sun. Patty manages to pick up a few things—that Garrett's father made his money in cement, that his mother has her own business, putting famous painters on greeting cards. Nothing that Patty can really use, though. Just as she's trying to explain for the fifth time what she does with computers, she notices a heavy older woman struggling to rise from a chaise beside the pool. "Little Bart!" the woman calls.

"Shit," Garrett whispers. Then, louder, "Hello, Mrs. Moss." Patty follows him as he drags his feet toward the pool.

The woman reaches up and hugs Garrett. "It's nice to see one familiar face." She's out of place here, with her cheap straw hat and speckled eye bags. "Where are those crazy parents of yours?"

He shrugs. "This is Patty, my wife."

"Wife!" Mrs. Moss gapes at Patty, then composes herself and winks. "Well, dear, you sure have yourself a handful."

"I sure have," Patty says.

"I've known Little Bart since he fell off his first bike. Could I tell you stories!"

Patty grins, barely able to believe her own luck. But before she can frame a single question, Garrett takes her hand and pulls her into the pool, silk blouse, skull shorts, and all.

Under the terms of his treatment, Garrett must accomplish one positive act each day. This may be anything from shaving to skydiving, but he must mindfully carry it out and log it in a journal. Garrett takes the responsibility very seriously. Every night before bed he makes his notation and hands the notebook to Patty. "Hiked downtown. Visited Vietnamese church. Made Patty's dinner. Went to group."

He contributes to his support as best he can, tending bar one week, playing in a friend's band the next. At home he meditates, irons, waits for Patty. Late at night he searches the TV channels for angry preachers and nature documentaries. He'll find an hour of jackals and hyenas, then pace until three in the morning, saying things like, "Fear is the natural state of our planet," and asking Patty if she would eat his dead body on a desert island. He gives her permission and lies mournfully on his back, waiting.

His body torments him; it's betrayed him too many times. Sometimes Patty sees him stretched out motionless on the couch, looking down the length of himself as if wondering how to sneak off undetected.

In the back of the journal of positive acts, upside-down, Garrett makes notes about Patty:

"The braces on her teeth prove she's a secret optimist."

"She would eat my body if we were stranded, but probably only to save it from wild animals."

"She wakes up watching me."

Back and forth he swims, his eyes fixed on the black bottom of the pool. Patty crouches in the shallow end, sunk up to her nostrils like a crocodile, plotting how to get Mrs. Moss aside and find out what happened to Garrett. The caterers are setting out platters heaped with crab claws that look delicious and smell like the rotten darkest caverns of the sea. Anyhow, Patty's allergic. They've been here almost two hours, and the Sundays still haven't appeared. No one seems to mind, least of all Garrett, amusing himself with a dead man's float. His scars don't show that much in bright sunlight. Bart Junior.

She tugs on his limp arm. "Let me put more sun block on."

He sits up and patiently waits while she spreads the cream across his shoulders.

"So where do you suppose your parents went?" For the thousandth time since they got married, Garrett shrugs. For the hundredth time, her fingers try to read the Braille of his back. "That's strange, to skip your own party, don't you think?"

"Patty." He pulls free, slides back into the black water. "Don't start."

Patty took the streetcar every day, so she was used to tunnel stalls. When the 5:45 outbound car shuddered and died under the river, she knew that in a few minutes an abrupt grinding would begin and the train would push its way out into the warm June evening. The other passengers were less sanguine; they muttered and pushed in the crowded aisle. Patty's breasts were pressed against the shoulder blades of the boy ahead of her. He was pulling his matted black hair and shifting from boot to boot, and when the lights went out, as they always did, Patty could feel his muscles thrumming as he wound himself tighter and tighter. She didn't understand this anxiety. She worked in a cubicle and lived in an apartment complex flanked by self-storage rentals, and these rush-hour intimacies had become almost pleasant.

The streetcar heaved, the lights flashed on again, and she saw that the boy had turned around so he was looking at her. His eyes were the muted green of weeds and jade, and he was not a boy but a man her own age. He was biting his lower lip very hard. "It's all right," she said, "we're moving now."

When she got off at the next stop, he was walking beside her, grinning despite his wounded lip. He said, "I like the sound your heels make, like there's nothing you don't know."

"I don't know much, but I can keep my head in an emergency."

"You'd be good on a desert island. Want some pancakes?"

They traded bites of Belgian waffles and inspected each other's bodies. He asked about her braces; she asked about the scar on his neck. She told him about the vampire canines her father couldn't afford to fix. He described his assorted lost battles with glass and gravity, his delicate new sobriety, the importance of saying yes.

"I like to watch you eat," he said. "You don't pretend you aren't hungry."

No one had ever enjoyed Patty quite so much. No beat-up body was ever so cheerful and free of regret. She married him three weeks later.

He's only gotten hurt once since then. Not long after the wedding: They'd been arguing about whether to get renters' insurance to cover the computer and guitars. He hadn't wanted to talk about it; she'd complained that he didn't care about their future. Just an idle newlywed accusation, but two hours later, drying the dishes, Garrett somehow managed to impale his bare foot on a barbecue skewer. The medical deductible was expensive. They still don't have renters' insurance.

Mrs. Moss's straw hat covers her face as she leans back on the chaise. So far, she and Patty have talked about skin cancer, bread machines, warehouse clubs, annoying telemarketers, and the probable cost of washing a glass-sided house.

"You know, Patty, I crashed this party. I caught Martha mailing invitations at the post office, and she had to be polite and ask me. There's not a soul here I know. But Martha always said her favorite thing in life was starting fresh."

"I've never met her," Patty says, looking around for Garrett, who went in to the bathroom twenty minutes ago. "Garrett doesn't say much about her, or his father."

"Well. Families are families."

"Not always," Patty says. She waits for a response. To her amazement, the straw hat begins to snore.

For ten minutes Patty listens to Mrs. Moss sleep or, possibly, pretend to sleep. Finally, she gives up and goes in to look for Garrett. She checks the kitchen and the den, she knocks on the downstairs bathroom door, but she can't find him.

The Sundays' house is too bright inside. You'd have to be blind to like it. She can imagine her father's reaction to such extravagance: "All that heat leaking out, and you're inviting robbers in," shaking his crew-cut head, wiping the dinner table with the experienced hand of a widower. After the wedding he talked to Garrett on the phone, ten minutes of weather and car maintenance, then he told Patty that her old room would always be waiting for her. His present to them was a ten-pound volume titled *Handling the Home Emergency*.

Patty shivers in her wet clothes. Despite the sun, it's cold in here. She's not just looking for Garrett, she's looking for clues, but her eyes can't get a grip. There are no photographs, no historic knickknacks, nothing to tell her what came before. Upstairs is darker and even colder. Made bold by the silence, Patty begins to investigate the guest rooms, sliding open closets and drawers, finding only sachets, padded hangers, and boxes of note cards covered with Impressionist babies. The aggressive blandness is so blinding that she almost misses a low shelf on the back wall of the smallest room, where someone has built a shrine to Garrett.

There's a jackknife, a plaster arm cast covered with childish autographs, a popsicle-stick jail holding a pipe-cleaner prisoner, and a framed school portrait, all arranged on a Cub Scout neckerchief. In the picture Garrett is eight or nine, bow-tied and big-eared, and although he's smiling, his upper teeth are planted in the meat of his small lower lip. She knows that smile; he still uses it today.

Patty hunches by the shelf for a long time, memorizing the boy in the picture, inferring cruelties, assigning blame, until her eyes feel sour and hot and she thinks she hears a noise. She gets up and peers into the hall, but the only sound is the murmuring party. There's one more closed door, across the landing. She pushes it open, softly, and stops short.

A man and a woman are standing beside a window, peering through sheer curtains at the crowd on the patio below. They're wearing pale, partyish outfits and holding matching glasses of something clear. The room smells of ripe garbage and Chanel No. 5.

"Too skinny," the woman is saying.

"Too god-awful stubborn," the man says.

Lightly, Patty knocks on the door frame. Only the man turns around.

"I'm Patty," she says, nicer than she means to be.

"Patty," he says, as if there could be no sillier name. "What did you do to that kid of ours?"

All she can do is stare, and open and close her hands.

"That's a joke," Mr. Sunday says. He grins for emphasis, showing a grayer version of Garrett's teeth, and closes the door upon her.

On her way downstairs Patty picks up the school picture of Garrett and sticks it down the front of her shorts. They have to get out of here.

Garrett is stretched out on Mrs. Moss's vacated chaise, telling a dozen people how he overcame drugs and met his wife. In this version, the stalled streetcar is a claustrophobic horror and Patty not merely sensible but heroic. Patty knows she should be pleased, but she detects something cool and mocking in Garrett's tone. While he talks he gradually pulls his legs back so that he's holding his ankles in his hands, and although the innocent observer might assume that Garrett is feeling relaxed, Patty knows what this posture means. He's holding his body down, before it can get him into trouble again.

His audience—golfers, Junior Leaguers, cholesterol-counters—can never understand him, but they try, smiling, nodding. Garrett has this effect upon people. At first they disdain him, then they want to feed him and get his blessing.

People ask him about drug treatment and city life. Finally, someone says, "What happened to your leg?"

"This?" He taps the pearly seam that zigzags down his left calf. "Just an accident."

"And here?" A woman shyly touches a claw mark on his shoulder.

"An accident, obviously," Patty says.

Garrett pushes his sunglasses back up his nose. "Patty doesn't believe in accidents. So." He noisily slaps himself on the chest. "I take full responsibility. It was all my fault."

Patty murmurs, "Nothing was your fault."

Now it's his turn to snort. "Patty, give me some credit."

She sits there for a while with a fake smile on her face, but the picture frame is digging into her stomach and Garrett's peevish mood has hurt her feelings. As soon as she inconspicuously can, she picks up her purse and heads back to the house to complete her theft. On the way she encounters Mrs. Moss, who's getting ready to leave.

"Patsy, it was a wonderful surprise to meet you," Mrs. Moss says. "Believe me, you're a miracle worker. If you see Bart and Martha—"

"I did," Patty says. "They were drinking. They smell bad."

"They don't drink."

Desperate now, Patty takes the older woman's wrist. "Tell me what they did to him."

"Why are you asking me? Who knows what I remember?" Mrs. Moss shakes Patty off. "Anyway, he's fine now. Off the dope and married, and he's even gained a little weight."

Patty holds the picture to her abdomen. "He weighs one hundred and twenty-five pounds, which would be fine if he weren't six feet tall."

"People here have been wondering what you feed him." Mrs. Moss pauses to let the injustice of this remark sink in. "If he can stand whatever happened, why can't you?" She jams on her straw hat and leaves through the side yard.

Once more Patty starts to go inside the house, and once more she is stopped, this time by the sight of Garrett himself, standing in the kitchen with his mother. She has dyed black hair and a long white dress, and she's trying to tell him something. He leans against the wall, looking down, apparently oblivious to the telephone pressing into his back.

Patty stands on the other side of the wall, straining to watch and listen. She can't make out Mrs. Sunday's face, she can't hear what she's saying, but when she sees her raise a hand, Patty bangs loudly on the glass. By the time she rushes inside, Garrett's mother has evaporated.

He bounces his hip bone against the edge of the counter. He won't look at Patty. The kitchen is full of crab shells, meat, and liquor bottles.

"I just wanted to make sure you were all right." Her knuckles hurt from hitting the glass. She puts them in her mouth, against the chafing but familiar metal of her braces.

"Patty, you don't know anything," he mutters.

She reaches out to touch his arm, but he snatches it away. "It's mine," he says.

"What?"

"Me. My body. It's mine, not yours. Remember that." He pokes himself in the chest a few times and walks out of the kitchen.

Patty turns in a furious circle, surrounded by the scalding glass, but there is no witness to her pain except a raw chicken, which she slaps so hard that it skids across the counter and tumbles on to the floor.

Blindly, she wanders through the side yard, the glass wall on one side, a prickly shrub on the other. Her brain is blaring with insult and frustration. She walks directly into Bart Sunday, Senior, who is standing between two rose bushes with his face pressed against the dining room window, peering at something inside.

They both lose their balance and fall into the sharp bushes, crying out. They both get up with long, bleeding scratches on their arms.

"Thanks, friend," Mr. Sunday says. He appears to be squeezing his wrist so that it bleeds harder. Patty looks away, nauseated, but the house just throws their reflections back at her.

He says, "I was looking for that son of mine."

Before she can stop herself, Patty says, "He's mine."

"'I don't want him, you can have him, he's too fat for me.' You've heard that polka song. You're a Polish girl, aren't you?" Patty sees that Garrett's father is completely sober, and this confuses her as much as his non sequiturs. He says, "I don't know what the hell I am, neither does Martha. Nobody kept track. And me, I never see my own kid. He's probably given you an earful."

He wants to know what she knows.

She could use this. She could talk to him, pick up a few bits of information, maybe trade a little of what she has for some of his vast treasure. But suddenly she wants only to protect what is hers and Garrett's, and to take a little revenge.

"I know everything," she says.

"Well, now." He rubs his wounded wrist, reaches down, and picks a round white stone from the walkway. "Bart told me you're the brains in the house. Let's see if you can break this window."

"That's not necessary."

"Come on." He presses the stone into her palm.

"I don't want to."

"Do it." He jogs her elbow, hard, and once again she smells that combination of perfume and trash. She breaks free of him and hurls the stone, which thuds dully against the window and drops into a low hedge, just below Garrett's staring face.

"It's not glass," Mr. Sunday says. "It's the latest thing."

When the Sundays finally appear at their party, a chilly breeze is rising. Mr. Sunday makes a loud, lame excuse about migraines while his wife stands beside him, stiff and swaying, her face turned toward the house. Patty has given up trying to make sense of anything. She floats in the warm pool water, ignored by one and all. God knows where Garrett is; the picture, however, is wrapped in a guest towel and hidden in the bottom of her bag.

Suddenly, there's a collective big-top gasp; Garrett is climbing out of a second-story window, on to the low, sloping roof that juts over the pool area. Gingerly, he picks his way across the rough shingles to the very edge, where he looks down at the pool, or maybe at the concrete deck, Patty can't tell. He's only ten or twelve feet up, but he's so small and alone up there that her ears start ringing.

She looks at the Sundays; they look back at her. Garrett looks down at all of them. He bends his knees and springs off the roof, clasping himself into a missile. In that moment, seeing her husband's bones suspended over the concrete, Patty wonders how she will ever single-handedly know the right way to live.

He hits the deep end of the pool hard, sending up a geyser that splashes Patty in the face. People clap and whistle, but Patty waits, coughing, while Garrett's body floats on the black bottom of the pool. Three, five seconds pass. Just as Patty starts to duck under the water, Garrett surfaces, popping up right in front of her, grinning and spitting water.

His parents have gone back inside the house.

When they get home, Garrett is silent, not angry anymore but subdued, soft from water and sun. He collapses on their unmade bed. Patty sees that the sun block didn't quite cover him; his chest and arms are scattered with little scalded brush strokes.

"It doesn't hurt," he says. "Come lie down with me." Calm and alert, his eyes move over her. "Did I scare you when I took that jump?"

"It was very reckless." Twelve times a day Patty swallows her father's voice; this time she sets it free. "It was as if you wanted to hurt yourself."

He barely bothers to shake his head. "If I wanted to hurt myself, I could've jumped on to the concrete really easy."

"Goddamn it." She punches her palm, although she'd like to tear her hair. "Just the fact that you could calculate something like that—"

"I wouldn't hurt you, Patty."

"I want you not to hurt *you*."

"I'm careful." He's watching her, adding her up: nagging nerves, fat-ass worries. Sometimes she forgets that he can see her, too. "Aren't I careful?" She shrugs. "I am. Careful, now. For both of us." He closes his eyes. Patty says, "Why did we go there today? Was it just one of your positive acts?"

"Don't say *just* a positive act. But it was. And I wanted to see the new house."

"It was awful."

"Yeah."

Patty is tempted to push for more, ask about the house he grew up in, but he's tired, and she's tired, and what use could she make of this information? Whom could she punish? If he can stand what happened, why can't she?

"She was after me to go upstairs and see something," he murmurs, on the edge of sleep.

"Your mother?"

"Mm. She'd made something for me."

"A positive act."

"Mmm."

"Will we have to go back there?"

But he's begun to sleep. With Garrett there's no falling involved, only a raftlike loosening and drifting. He seems to have no grudges to hold him back.

Patty watches him for a few minutes, then she opens her bag and unwraps the stolen picture. Outside the open window she can hear the neighbors fighting their usual fight—she says he cheats, he says she's crazy. At the same time, in another apartment, shy fingers are wandering on a piano. She sets the picture on the nightstand, but it looks out of place amid the computer printouts and guitar strings, and the wedding-day snapshot of Patty and Garrett, riding a streetcar in their brightest clothes. She decides to hide the picture in a safe place, on her bookshelf, behind *Handling the Home Emergency*, which Garrett has never opened.

The neighbor's piano kicks into something jazzy, sweet and dirty. Garrett turns on to his stomach, smiling. All night he'll flip back and forth, working his legs, bracing against her, kicking the wall.

Again she sees him standing on the roof, measuring the distance to safety, deciding not to hurt himself. Although she knows she should let him keep floating into sleep, her body is telling her to lay herself across him, not as a nurse, an owner, or a carnivore, not as a mother or a foxhole buddy, but simply as an admirer.

She'll do that. But first she lays a finger on one of the oldest scars, supposedly from a teenage fall from a roller coaster, now shrunken and unreadable like a rearview highway sign. The scar will never disappear. Garrett's body always will frighten her. But it's faith outrunning history. It's the greatest story ever told. It's his.

Everglade

Carol's father was filling his house with snakes.

She caught him one July afternoon, crouched in the remains of his vegetable patch, forcing a squirming handful of stripes into his coat pocket. She backed away, into the house, where she found two more snakes tangled together on the reclining chair. Another lay on the television top, sunning itself in a fat gray ring.

Because she had always feared and pitied her father, far into his old age and her own years of doubt and fatigue, it cost her great effort to say, "Dad, do you want that snake on the TV?"

He hung the coat from a peg, where it twisted with angry life. He said, "Here in Miami, we milk serpents for their venom."

We're in New Hampshire, Carol told herself. That night she called her brother in Honolulu.

Philip said, "I suppose he could have gone to Miami at some point. And he's always liked snakes, so, frankly, I don't see the harm."

"Frankly" was one of Philip's favorite expressions, along with "I'm as guilty as anyone," which he didn't use this time.

Carol was certain that her father had never been to Florida, or anywhere. He'd even hated going to town. But she and Philip were lifelong allies, so she didn't insist upon what she'd seen; she just said, "Goodnight, and kiss your boy for me."

"Kiss your girls."

Her daughters were long grown and gone, but she knew what he meant. They had struggled to be good parents. To make their children happy, Carol and Philip had given up savings, rest, even their spouses. Now, hardest of all, they demanded nothing in return.

That night Carol twisted in her bed and tried to remember when her father had started to disappear. Last winter, she'd noticed, he stopped shoveling out from under snowstorms. He took to sitting guard on the rough ice of his back steps, convinced that the neighbor's dog, a quarter mile away, was about to break its chain and trespass. Never before had he shown interest in the neighbors. Carol thought he must be lonely since her mother's death. Then he began loading his hatband with bullets. One April day she found him standing on the property line of his farthest field, watching the dog leap, spring-drunk, on its tether. Her father was hooked on a piece of fence wire; the melting snow had soaked him to his knees. Afraid to insult him with questions, Carol said nothing. As she knelt in the fragrant slush, squinting, trying to free him, he touched her hair, lightly, and said in another man's voice, "Poor thing."

Now she rubbed her eyes and said, "He's gone." She tried to mourn, but her grief kept striking the hard curb of disbelief. He couldn't go, because he had always been there, no matter how hard she'd tried to look away.

Two days after discovering the snakes, Carol drove back out to the farm and stood, spying, in the tall grass outside the parlor window. She was trying to see her father as a sad old man.

He was sitting in the recliner, ankles close together, inspecting a thick picture album. His hair was white and soiled, and his cheeks had fallen into elderly clumps, but despite this evidence, and despite the words she whispered to herself—"sad," "old"— she could not overlook the selfish angle of his spine.

"It's hard for him," her mother used to say. She'd died a year ago, in her bed upstairs, and although she'd asked to be buried in the town cemetery with everyone else, he'd had her cremated. Then he never mentioned her again. Carol had been quietly searching the property for her mother's ashes but so far had gotten no farther than the parlor and the toolshed. She imagined a lacquered canister, heavy, cool, and conclusive. She planned to take it home and hide it. Once she had the ashes, she thought, she'd be able to forgive the cremation. Now, with snakes slipping through every room of the house, she knew she'd never have the courage to keep looking.

When Carol knocked on the front door, her father greeted her with the easy warmth of a stranger. Cautiously, she stepped inside, alert to slithering movement.

"Since we got to Miami, we haven't had a moment to ourselves," he said. "Tomorrow we go to the Everglades."

She'd bought a sack of fast food for his dinner, so she wouldn't have to open any cupboards. As she served him, he said, "The sun is crazy strong, but it's not worth it to buy dark glasses if you aren't going to stay. Where's your husband, ma'am?"

"Lord knows," she said, pretending to be lighthearted, not bitter and literal.

"Chased out by those girls of yours, I bet."

This remark was so much like Carol's real father that she flinched and stepped back from the table.

He was insisting. "Am I right?"

She could neither argue nor change the subject. She couldn't even think about the snakes. She could only stand there, remembering.

First, he would complain about a mess in the house—a slight disorder of towels or forks, the natural tangle of a family. Next, he would complain about Carol and Philip and the central fact of children themselves—always taking, taking—then, finally, he would condemn his wife for loving the children best. Her mother never argued back, just turned her face away from all of them, blushing with the strain of impartiality.

She had been sweet, clumsy, nervous, and shy. When they were little, they'd adored her and pushed him away. Then they got older and felt sorry and over-praised everything he did for them, from Christmas trees to garden beans. Proud and wary, he retreated to the toolshed. In the evenings they would peer over their schoolbooks to watch him watch their mother. Things got worse and worse. "He feels left out," her mother once said. When Philip replied, "He should," she slapped both children. Jealousy, not pain, made them wail.

Philip and Carol stuffed their own children with favors and hope and triumphantly paraded them before their grandfather, who shrugged and went back to his work.

Now he was gesturing with his plastic fork, expansive again, a wise traveler. "Don't worry about catching a man," he told Carol. "You're old enough to walk alone."

"Oh, I'm not worried. I asked him to go. He wasn't cut out for raising children. Now here I am stuck in Miami." She could not resist adding, "You must miss your wife."

"She's in the garden."

"Mama?" she said, for the first time in a year.

Her father dropped his head and concentrated on his chicken nuggets, pushing and digging, wearing the stubborn face of a man who knows he's made a serious mistake.

For a few minutes Carol could do nothing but sit there, opening and closing her hands, staring into the adjoining parlor, at the picture album he'd left on the arm of his chair. Then she went out to the garden.

Her first thought was to make a bouquet, but although the weeds were shaped like flowers, with shiny stems and funnel-shaped blossoms, they were knotted fast in the ground. Carol twisted and pulled, remembering her father's back curved over neat rows, his rusty laborer's smell when he returned to the house with a hat full of peas. She knew that his tools still hung, corroded but well-ordered, in the shed. He must wander all day now, imagining that he was fixing things. She pulled hard on the weed stem, straining her ankles and knees, remembering. Eventually, she noticed the short green snake by her left foot.

To her own surprise, she was neither frightened nor disgusted. For once she felt too big and old for that. Wearily, feeling the reproach of her middle-aged back, she bent and picked up the snake. She dangled it before her eyes. It looked back at her with a calm, ancient face, refusing to blink or move, even after she tossed it toward the field.

"Go on." She nudged the snake with her foot. It moved two hesitant inches. "Go." Another inch. "Go." She heard the childish whine in her voice and stopped herself. What was she defending? She no longer lived here. Besides, the snake probably was sick; why else would it hang so close? She picked it up again and carried it to the house. She set it on the front steps, got in her car, and drove away. Long after dark that night, she lifted her weed-stained palm to her nose and breathed deeply. She whispered, "Walk alone."

Philip said, "I'm as guilty as anyone."

"Me too," Carol said. "But I still think it's kinder to leave him there."

"And, frankly, it's his house."

Then the oil delivery man came and found the basement full of snakes. The town ambulance carried Carol's father away, sedated like big game. She followed him to the Country Gentleman's Home with sport shirts and back issues of *Golden Traveler*. "Thanks a million," he said. "I think I'm going to break down and buy some dark glasses." She brought him a pair on her next visit.

After the doctor, lawyer, caseworker, and exterminator had left, assuring her that the snakes were gone and the house was her responsibility, Carol made herself sit in the recliner and pick up the picture album her father had been studying.

Inside she found many snapshots of Florida Indians, alligators, and water moccasins, all dated 1940, years before she was born. One thumb-worn picture fell into her lap: her mother, sitting alone in a small boat, looking out over the grassy swamp of the Everglades. Neither beautiful nor strong but turned away, and, in this slender moment of privacy, most exotic.

I'll Hold You Up

Laura and Ward picked each other out of the end-of-the-summer party, spent the night at her apartment, then decided to drive naked to the ocean, one hundred and fifty miles away. They had fallen in love.

They started too late to make good time. Labor Day traffic out of Washington was thick; Ward and Laura crawled along, as sweaty and frustrated as everyone else, as downtown slowly gave way to slums, warehouses, and suburbs. No one, not even truck drivers, noticed that the couple in the red Miata wore no clothes.

Laura wore her suit of sunlight easily. Her legs rubbed catlike against the velour car seat, and her inky hair lifted and streamed in the blowing air. Her eyes were closed against the noon glare because she'd refused to compromise her nakedness with sunglasses. To her dismay, Ward had insisted upon wearing his shoes, big gray hiking boots that clung to his ankles like twin buckets of cement. It was dangerous to drive barefoot, he said.

The summer had left Ward patched with color—conquistador brown on his shoulders and calves, newborn pink on his peeling cheekbones, drowned white around his hips. He steered with his hands set in the 10-to-2 driver's-ed position.

He said, "This is like those dreams where suddenly you're nude, but nobody sees you. But still you try to hide."

"I don't try to hide," Laura said, loftily, lying.

She was in a faint bad humor, partly because of her hangover, which had left her jittery and ashamed, and partly because her leavened mood of the dawn had burned away. The holiday was a grinding machine. They were pressed on every side by speedboats, jet skis, pickup trucks loaded with beer kegs and dogs, everyone hurtling toward the shore for the last day of summer.

She twisted the ruby ring she'd bought herself, with a promise to do well, when she'd moved to Washington the year before. She was trying to remember, through all the wind and highway fumes, the moment just before sunrise when she knew she was in love. Laura didn't doubt the moment, but she was having trouble locating it.

She must have looked worried, because Ward reached over the gear shift and took her hand, just for a second. By silent mutual consent they pulled apart. They were shy. They didn't know each other.

It had been the last party of the season, at the Georgetown condo of somebody's friend. There were Hawaiian shirts, tequila shooters, "Louie, Louie" played thirteen times on four pairs of speakers. That late in the season, most people were too tired to meet anyone new, so they hung in their habitual work cliques. They all worked hard, in government offices and law firms, at jobs they hoped soon to rise above. They were all turning thirty, to their own surprise.

Laura always felt anxious at Labor Day, when the year took a perceptible downward drop into grayness, chill, and New Year's resolutions. Nothing heralded the arrival of this bleak season more than the muscular dystrophy telethon. So when the party hostess insisted that everyone gather around her bedroom TV to watch the first few moments of the show, Laura hung back in the living room, alone, hiding from Jerry Lewis and his nervous, bitter eyes.

She drank a beer. She ate a taco. She eavesdropped on the laughter in the next room. Then she noticed the man on the balcony. He was soft-shouldered but tall; his white shirttails were loose, and he was stretching out his arms like seagull wings.

Laura crept up to the other side of the balcony door and saw that he was playing airplane. Passenger jets were descending overhead, low and heavy, on their approach down the Potomac to the airport; he was helping them land, pressing down the air with his palms, dipping his knees. A boyish rag of hair hung on his collar. Laura thought he must be someone's disturbed brother, until she noticed the expensive crumpling of his shirt and the complex laces of his hiking boots.

She stood behind the door, studying him, with the sinking sun in her eyes and Jerry Lewis cackling at her back. When he turned and saw her, she was smiling, in pure relief.

Summer wasn't over yet.

Laura was the one who wanted to ride naked to the shore. They took her car, but Ward had agreed to drive, just as he had agreed to skip breakfast and not to tell her about himself, not yet.

Laura hadn't wanted to drive because she'd wanted no distraction from her first day in love in more than a year. She thought that the car trip with Ward would be one long quiver of desire. But as soon as they hit traffic, their heads started to ache. Their genitals, so large and commanding in the dark, shrank in the daylight until they could barely be seen amid all the workaday limbs.

This surprising lack of lust gave Laura plenty of time to think, but it was difficult to think through her hangover and hard to watch the passing scenery through the scalding sunlight. She hung her head and inspected her body, which was overexposed and line-free in the brightness. She did daily exercises to keep tight. Ward was long-boned but a bit loose around the middle. He had soft baby hair and a habit of patting his chest, or maybe his heart, every few minutes. Laura kept sweeping him with her eyes, trying to harvest lovable details, but she could not stop noticing his heavy, tightly laced boots.

They hadn't talked much at the party. Mainly, they'd stood at the edges of other people's conversations, smiling at one another. Later, they walked the long way back to her apartment, weaving through the darkening, dangerous streets. Ward began to offer the usual career and romantic information, but Laura pinched his lips shut. "None of this matters yet," she said, and he agreed that what mattered was them, that moment. They bought a bottle of strawberry wine and a pack of Marlboros, and they walked along

holding hands and blowing amateur smoke rings. They pretended that they were strolling through Laura's brain, that the cars
were her thoughts and the wires were her nerves, then she said,
"No, it's my heart," so Ward closed his eyes and walked a whole
block of sidewalk without stepping on a crack. In gratitude, Laura
turned a shaky cartwheel, called up from her cheerleading days.
Ward responded with a yodel and a handspring. Laura tightrope-
walked down a low spiked fence, six steps, then she jumped into
Ward's arms and he twirled her around like a baby or a toy plane
before setting her on his shoulders, which were soft but broad.
She rode there the rest of the way home, high above him, grabbing at tree branches and their tough, late-summer leaves.

"Laura?" He spoke her name experimentally, tasting it. "We
forgot to sleep last night."

She was watching housing developments slowly surrender to
cornfields and truck stops. They were halfway there. "I haven't
really slept since college."

"Ha!" He tapped her arm. "I caught you telling a fact. That
means I can tell you one."

"One." She shifted her sweaty thighs on the velour.

"OK." He considered, patting his heart. "I've had three jobs in
three states in three years." He waited for her to ask for details.
She only nodded and turned back to the window.

Every time it began the same, with these eager, proffered facts,
and ended the same, in confusion and reproach. What good
would it do him to know that she had been engaged twice and
spent her days writing press releases for the gravel association?
What mattered—that her job frightened her, that somehow in
the past year the tables had turned and now her mother was
calling *her* to cry and complain—these things could not be told
to a new lover, not yet.

What difference did it make if he liked to fly, hated asparagus,
was an aspiring lobbyist or a disillusioned Democrat? It was
much nicer to contemplate the whole man, his cellophane wrap
unbroken, his hopes and history neatly arranged inside him like
rows of imported chocolates.

This was Laura's theory. In practice, she was unable to see Ward as a whole man, as an agreeable man, or even as the boyish helper of planes. She could only see him as a foot, lazily riding the accelerator of her car. They were stuck in the slow lane, their front view blocked by the square behind of a Winnebago, even though there was plenty of room to pass.

If only they could be there.

They had clutched each other, hearts galloping, lungs beating; they had risen on their own hot dry chant, *I love you I love you*, until the room was full and stretched like a balloon and they couldn't stand it anymore, they burst naked out of her apartment into the bright, airy day. They had laughed and pushed each other forward, yelping as their bare feet struck the pavement. They ran for her car and drove three blocks before they thought to go back for some money and clothes, and Ward's boots.

Now the sun was slipping behind the car, and Laura was back in the shadows. The lines had reappeared on her neck and wrists. Her body looked like any other outfit, and tomorrow she had to write another press release on another issue she didn't understand. Out her window she saw the same vegetable stands, mockingly repeating themselves; the same truck stops, the same slow-creeping Winnebago—

"Ward?" She touched the skin of his shoulder, felt him flinch beneath her strange touch. "Let me drive."

That was better. She drove seventy-five miles an hour, her spirits rising as the speed drilled up through the sole of her foot.

Ward did his best not to betray alarm at her driving, but he managed at every turn to sneak in unspoken facts about himself. When they passed some bicyclists, he pumped his fist at them in a fraternal salute. He tuned in a radio opera and sang the party song from *La Traviata* in what sounded like genuine Italian.

Laura was just starting to get annoyed when she passed an accident and he begged her to stop the car. "We'd better help them," he said.

"*Ward*." She pointed at his bare crotch.

"I'll put on a towel. You can stay in the car."

"The police are already there." But she pulled off the highway and backed up on the gravelly shoulder.

A silver sports car lay in the ditch weeds, upside down and faintly smoking. A state trooper was leaning down to talk to a young woman who was sitting in the dirt with her curly head in her hands. She looked unhurt but heartbroken. Laura watched Ward tighten the pink beach towel around his waist, stride up to the wreck, and offer his help. Both the girl and the trooper waved him away without looking at him. Ward hesitated at the edge of the accident for a moment, then he picked up a plastic cooler from the belongings scattered in the ditch. He walked up to the girl, who still stared down at the dirt, and quietly set the cooler at her feet.

Back in his seat, he peeled off the towel and shyly smiled at his kneecaps. "I guess that was pretty stupid."

"In a good way." Laura smiled at the side of his face and stepped on the gas.

Passing by a shopping plaza in Maryland, she got an idea. "Are you hungry?" she said.

"No, my stomach's still a little weak from the shooters."

"I'm going to try something." She made a U-turn and pulled up to the drive-through window of a Burger King, where she ordered twelve dollars' worth of food and received it without a glance from the cashier. Next, she stopped at a bank and hobbled twenty feet across a gravel lot to withdraw cash from the machine. Again, nobody seemed to notice. "Don't people see anything but themselves?" Laura asked Ward, exasperated.

"I do," he said. He laid a tentative palm on her thigh, but she was determined; she got back on the highway, pushed the car up to eighty, and didn't slow down until she saw a picnic area by the side of the road.

Ward said, "Is this smart?"

"Who cares?" She pushed open her door, gathering up a stadium blanket and the Burger King bag. "I'm hungry and hot, and I guess we know we're invisible. And it's still goddamn summer."

Ward waited for a truck to pass, darted out of the car, and dove on to the blanket, which Laura had spread on a bristly patch of grass. There wasn't much to the picnic area, just a peeling table, a cold campfire, and an embankment down to an evaporated river.

"We aren't going to make it to the beach," he said.

"I don't mind. I just wanted the ride, didn't you?" Laura was happy to be outside, even though cars were flying past them with blind indifference. She picked apart a cheeseburger and fed it to Ward. He let her take off his boots and rub his feet, which were long and surprisingly delicate. He pressed his thumb against her shoulder, watched his white print dissolve on a field of scarlet. "You're burning up," he said. Then, "I can't remember why we're doing this."

"Because we're madly in love."

"Oh. Right."

They laughed. Laura stretched out, listening to crows and traffic. "I liked what you did for that girl back there. And I liked you yesterday, with the planes."

"Eeh." He pulled his forearm up to hide his face. "I was pretty drunk."

"You're kind without having to stop and think about it. But I was drunk too."

"I can't drink anymore. I shouldn't."

"Me neither."

They fell asleep pressed together, heedless of the dropping sun and the rising breeze. Laura dreamed the ocean had her in its warm salt clutch and was bouncing her, rocking her; she was a baby fish, then an old shell-bone. Then she was plummeting through cold air onto a field of iron spikes.

She twisted and opened her eyes and saw a charred stick jabbing her shoulder, wielded by a hook-necked old woman in a heavy coat. "I thought you were dead," the woman said, calmly. "I said, 'Randall, only two dead people could enjoy this wind.'" A spotted old man stood behind her. He was also dressed for winter, in a hunting jacket and flap-eared cap. A fat dachshund squirmed in his arms.

"Aren't you cold?" the woman said.

Ward tried to cover himself with the edge of the blanket. Laura glared at the intruders, proud and defiant. "We have nothing to be ashamed of," she said.

"Not yet, I'm sure you don't," the woman said. "We don't mind, do we, Randall?"

The man kicked Ward's bare ankle. "Far from it."

The old people sat down at the picnic table, pulled out a thermos and a stack of sandwiches, and began to eat, taking very large bites, while their dog trotted over to Laura and Ward. It was prickly and plump, and it smelled bad. Laura screamed softly when it tried to lie across her legs. The woman looked over and laughed. "Barney, are you getting fresh with that poor girl?"

"We should go," Ward said.

"No way." Laura moved closer to Ward, away from the dog, which lay in a panting tube on the grass.

The old people concentrated upon their food and did not seem to give the naked young couple another thought. Still, Laura and Ward began to feel embarrassed by their bodies. Ward put up a hand to cover his bald spot, a velvety pink patch the size of a poker chip. Laura suddenly worried that her bottom sagged, and rolled over to hide it.

I'll hold you up. That was it, the moment she had been trying to remember. They'd been tangled together at the foot of her bed, lost in the dark. She'd said, "I'm afraid," and he'd said, "I'll hold you up"—urgently, promising—and she'd believed him.

A cool wind was sweeping up trash and leaves and campfire grit. Laura's burned skin made her shiver. She wanted the ocean, the warm one she'd just dreamed about.

The old people finished their meal. They brushed off crumbs, kissed each other on the mouth, called Barney, and drove away without so much as a glance at Laura and Ward.

Silently, they put their clothes on, crouched by the side of the car, concealed from the road. Ward put on his stale party clothes from the day before, but Laura had brought a new sunsuit she'd found in the juniors department—gum-pink with a pattern of beach balls and surfboards. When she saw Ward staring at the outfit, she wanted to cross her arms over her chest and hide herself. But she only sighed and shrugged.

"It's all right," he said. "I like it."

This hollow, husbandly lie touched her, in a different way from the sidewalk antics of the night before. "I've changed my mind again," she said. "I really need that ocean now."

He stopped stuffing his shirt into his jeans, glanced at the pink western sky. "It will be dark before we know it. And I have an early meeting tomorrow."

She rubbed her feverish arms. "We can make it back in plenty of time. I'll drive. Please."

He stroked the bright fabric of her sunsuit, soothing her, stalling.

The wind churned around them. "Please," she said. "You can tell me everything. Every job and girl and stupid thing you've done. And next time we'll do what you want."

"Next time, huh?" He knelt in the gravel to put on his boots, biting his tongue in concentration as he double-knotted the laces. He couldn't have looked clumsier or denser, but Laura started feeling it again, the low pulse of desire, marbled now with a strange tenderness that may have been pity.

Ward tied his right boot, saw her looking down at him.

"They're good for rough hikes. Maybe I'll take you, next time."

"Please," she said.

Go

When I look through my peephole and see the yellow happy face, my first thought is, "How did this get past security?" My building has a locked street door, a sharp-eyed doorman with a club on his belt, and a digitally coded elevator. Nothing bad can get in. The face is round and furry; it begins to croon my name. I back away from the door in real alarm. Should I call someone, Clyde the doorman, maybe? What do I tell him? I tiptoe back to the door and take another peek. The yellow face has fallen away, revealing a headful of crimson curls and, beneath them, the smile I know best.

"Mom!" I'm laughing as I struggle to pull open the door.

"I'm out of context," my mother gleefully says, and indeed she is, a beaming oddity in my sixty-watt hallway, wearing fuchsia lambswool in the early September heat, holding a suitcase in one hand and a smiley-face pillow in the other. She's supposed to be a thousand miles away. "But I wanted to surprise you on your birthday, and I certainly did!" Then, "You're glad, right?"

"You know that." I reach for her suitcase, bracing myself against my steel door, which is trying to slam shut on both of us. The suitcase is emerald-green leather, brand new.

"I have to go back tomorrow," she says. Before I can protest, she takes my face between her palms for a close examination. "Thirty-five years old!" Wincing, as if I've done something reckless. "Joy, you've cut your hair so short."

We saw each other ten months ago, when I went back home to Minneapolis, but she keeps holding my head, looking hard into my eyes as if the real me is wandering lost in there. I know how she feels. No matter how often I see her, I can't help thinking that this woman with the crumpled jaw line, waxy fingers, and

172

riotous wardrobe is not my real mother. My real mother was not a joker but a worrier, and she dyed her red hair brown.

"Joy," she sighs. "Joy, Joy, Joy." She gently knocks her forehead against mine each time she says my name.

"Mom, are you OK?"

"I'm better than that. I'm on my way."

"What does that mean?"

"I'll tell you all about it later."

"You're scaring me."

"Don't be. It's a good thing. Now!" She lets go of my head and rubs her hands together, grinning. "Where's my grandbaby?"

I can hardly bear to tell her that her grandbaby has a leak. She loves him so, almost as if he were real.

Actually, he's an inflatable plastic doll, fourteen inches high, modeled after Edvard Munch's *The Scream*. I got him three years ago from a catalog called "That's Not Funny: Irreverent Gifts for a Pompous World." He leaked from the start, and I should have sent him back, but I was delighted to wake up every morning and see the puckered pink face howling atop my dresser. And the leak was barely noticeable at first, just a slight leftward sag that I would correct every so often by blowing a little more air into his side. A few months ago the problem turned serious. Sometimes I would come home from work to find Scream toppled over, deflated, shielding his face with his arms as if he no longer had the strength to protest.

"Poor baby!" My mother has draped the doll over her shoulder and is pretending to burp him. There's barely room for all three of us in my kitchenette, but she wants to see my face as I unpack the things she's brought for me: a hefty jar of caviar, two bottles of Veuve Clicquot, pâté-stuffed quails, instant espresso powder, and one hundred Atomic Fireballs. "Where are you leaking from?"

"I can't tell." I've pressed him to my ear and listened; I've submerged him in water and studied his seams. "Now I have to refill him every day before I go to work."

I don't mind, though. If anything, the leak has made me feel more tender toward my poor Scream. Last month I went away for a few days with a potential boyfriend and came home to find the doll lying flattened on my bedroom floor. Immediate CPR was required. I sat on the bed, hunched over, blowing so intently that I didn't see my potential boyfriend watching me from the doorway. When I finally noticed him, I didn't even try to explain. "It's all right," he said, but neither of us laughed, and that was that. He was a zoning enforcement officer.

"I'm sure you made the right choice," my mother says. Her love for Scream is an ongoing joke between us, though I'm not sure exactly what it refers to. It doesn't really matter. For years she's been cultivating a carefree wackiness, and I don't begrudge her.

Now she says, "Let's go out and see the day." She's taken off her lambswool sweater, revealing a leotard covered with silk-screened eyeballs.

"Just let me find a place for the champagne," I say. My refrigerator is quite small. "Thank you, by the way."

"Did I tell you I quit drinking? I'll make an exception for tonight, though."

"You never drank much."

"Still. I woke up one morning and realized that time will knock me out soon enough. Until then, I might as well stay awake."

"You're scaring me again."

"It's nothing like that."

"What's nothing like that?"

"A surprise. Is that an electric log in your fireplace?"

"I'm afraid so."

This is my first venture into real estate, and I can tell she's disappointed by what two hundred thousand dollars has bought: seven hundred square feet, a windowless bathroom, unstainable gray nylon carpet, and low, curdled-looking ceilings. When I rented, I had character—leaded glass, wainscoting—but these days, for someone in my price range, character means a bad neighborhood. And this is, if not a great neighborhood, at least a respectable one. I'm flanked by apartment houses just like mine, and my windows face the bulging rear end of a Catholic church. The old stone building is squat and mottled with soot, but occasionally there's a night service and the stained glass glows, just a little, enough to make me stand and stare.

"Hurry up, sweetheart. We're losing the afternoon. And I want to get back and open your presents."

"OK." But I pause in the kitchenette, rubbing my neck, where an odd stiffness has taken hold. In my shoulders, too. Am I getting sick? Maybe it's just the fallout from my birthday. Thirty-five is a strange age, half empty, half full.

My mother holds Scream to her ear, squeezes. "I just filled you up, and already you're going soft."

"I told you."

"I guess Santa will have to bring a new one."

"No." The firmness in my voice surprises both of us. "He's fine the way he is."

"All right, I don't want to be a bossy grandma." She lifts the doll to eye level, winks at the bulb-shaped face. "But I have to say, I never thought of you as a 'he.'"

When I first saw the catalog with Scream, I was working for a tacky postcard company and dating a guy who designed bathtub toys for grown-ups. I lived for kitsch. My apartment was a museum of foolish, adorable junk: voodoo dolls, state fair ashtrays, jumbo rosaries, seashell crucifixions. I wore bowling shirts and saddle shoes; I was the most amusing person I knew. Then irony became a mainstream commodity, like cashmere and espresso beans. *The Scream* was snatched up by marketers and reproduced on everything from mouse pads to boxer shorts. Other pieces of art had gone this route, but *The Scream*'s sudden popularity was disconcerting. Did everybody share Munch's horror, or were they just sick of taking it seriously?

I began to notice something. *The Scream* fit less well with my life, and my life was changing without my consent. My clothes were turning duller of color, heavier of fabric. Passing mirrors, I was surprised by my own pursed, disapproving lips. Somehow I was working for a salt-processing company. When I bought this apartment, I didn't bother unpacking the voodoo dolls and rosaries; there wasn't enough room, once I'd arranged my clothes and books. Anyway, now that irony was everywhere, I was getting sick of it. Even though I knew it had rescued my mother.

For years she took things seriously. She had to. She was a divorced woman with a child to protect. So she bought low-heeled shoes and no-color lipstick and hesitated before she spoke, making sure of her grammar, afraid of sounding ignorant and loose. She went by Joan instead of her real name, Vanessa. Our house was the cleanest; our Buick, the best-waxed. My braids were tighter than anybody else's. Then I went off to college and started my own life and, slowly but bravely, my mother began to unfurl.

She took down the heavy curtains in our house, defying the Minnesota winters, craving light. She bought an opera season ticket and joined a hiking group. It was hard. Other people would confidently hold forth, dropping the names of mezzo-sopranos and migratory birds, and she would freeze, silenced by all she didn't know. How could she have known anything? She'd only worked and raised me.

But she stuck with it. She let her real red hair grow in. She quit her bank job and went to work for a company that made hot-air balloons. She took back her real name. Shy, always, when I came home, as if I (who had separate boyfriends for casual and dress-up) might disapprove.

Five years ago the last shackles burst.

She'd gone to the art museum to see an exhibit of Dutch religious paintings. Both the newspaper and her boss had said the show must not be missed. But my mother knew neither art nor religion. Even after buying a catalog and renting an audio guide, she was confounded by the cramped old canvasses. Virgin and child, again and again—why? And who were all those saints? She walked away defeated, stopping in the museum's gift shop for consolation, hoping to find a scarf or some nice note cards. She found the Mona Lisa's head on a cloth cat body.

She's described the moment to me at least ten times:

"I just stood there and stared. Somebody had nerve, to mess with the Mona Lisa! And suddenly I got it: Art wasn't any better than I was. I mean, it was only human. It was all right to laugh."

She bought the cat to remind herself of what she'd learned. One thing led to another. She acquired a Venus de Milo nightlight, a scowling-Beethoven cookie jar, a mobile strung with dead philosophers. Gradually, she expanded into popular culture: fat-Elvis Christmas ornaments, oven mitts shaped like old Cadillacs. And then she saw my Scream and fell in love ("It's so cute! You just want to pick it up and carry it around!"). She bought me a refrigerator magnet, an umbrella, and a pair of coffee mugs, all bearing the same horror-stricken face.

Back in Minneapolis, our old life was gone, replaced by funny, colorful things, except for my bedroom, which had been preserved in all its dotted swiss, maple wood, and dimness, an artifact of what we used to try to be.

We spend my birthday afternoon walking, and walking: up and down the city streets, past shops full of Fiestaware and platform shoes and Hawaiian shirts and Slinkys, past one cafe that serves only peanut butter sandwiches and another that serves only dog biscuits. "Where are the hospitals and old-folks homes?" my mother wants to know. "Not that I'm complaining."

She walks much faster than I do. "Keep moving, that's my motto these days," she says. Tired, still feeling that strange stiffness, I take her to the garden across the street from my building. It's tucked along the church's eastern flank—small, a little dark, with a shyly sputtering fountain and leggy clumps of impatiens. I take a seat on the only bench, while my mother examines the stone saints and crosses.

The church's side door is open, and old ladies are tottering into mass. They're wearing heavy coats, despite the heat. They don't seem to notice anything around them, not the low gray sky, not even the church itself.

"Now *they're* in context," my mother says. "There's not a doubt in their minds."

"God, I hope not. I hope by now they know what they're about."

She pats St. Joseph's lichen-speckled face. "I, on the other hand, will never live long enough to get this."

"Do you really have to leave tomorrow?"

"That's my surprise." She elbows me over on the bench. "I'm going on a trip." Could this be a euphemism for something awful? But she's smiling and waving her hands. "A grand tour, as they used to say. With Vincent. I told you about him, he used to break horses, now he owns that movie theater." I can't remember what she said, something about kind eyes and a big nose. "We're going to do Europe, Russia, India, maybe Japan. Starting three weeks from today. I've got my passport and my luggage. I sold the house. We close day after tomorrow, that's why I have to get back."

My mouth actually falls open. "What—"

She laughs. "It's a grand tour, I told you."

"What about your job?"

"As of last week, I'm officially retired."

"When are you coming back?"

"Who knows? Joy, I thought you'd be happy."

"I am." But I seem to be channeling the voice of an eight-year-old brat.

She says, "It's not as if you're used to seeing me every day. We're lucky to get together once a year."

"I know."

"Life goes on. We have to keep moving."

"I know!"

A low murmuring starts up inside the church, rolls out the open door, tamps down our not-quite-fight. I listen hard but can't make out the prayer. My mother says, "It's pretty, though, isn't it?"

I nod, unable to speak. Though I could cry, or scream, adult words are beyond me right now.

She asks, "Have you ever been inside?"

I manage to mutter, "Not yet."

When we stand up to leave, my left knee locks, and I almost topple into St. Joseph. My mother catches me and sets me upright, then bursts out laughing. "Joy, do you know what I'm thinking of?"

Despite myself, I have to smile.

I never knew why it happened or when it would happen next. Once on the first day of third grade, right after she'd dropped me off. Once when I was walking up to sit on Santa's lap at Dayton's department store. And at least a dozen other times, always in public places: I would lock up, rising onto the toes of my saddle shoes as if pulled up by my own tight braids, eyes wide, arms outstretched, fingers splayed and grasping. It would last five or ten minutes, and although I was frozen like something bewitched, I was never afraid. I liked to make things stop. That's what I called it, to myself, "stopping." It worried my mother, though. Whenever it happened, she would pick up my rigid body and carry me out of people's sight.

She took me to a specialist, handsome Dr. Collier, who ran tests and declared me healthy. "It's a phase she's bound to outgrow," he said. He was right. Eventually, I grew too big for my mother to drag to safety, and the stopping came to an end. It only happened once more, my first night away at college, but since there was nobody to help me, nobody who even knew me, the spell broke almost instantly.

She hands me the presents one at a time and eagerly watches me open them: a Gumby-and-Pokey desk lamp, chocolates shaped like Michelangelo's *David*, days-of-the-week panties, leggings patterned with King Tut's head.

"They came with a matching T-shirt that said, 'Stop Looking at My Tuts,' but I thought that was a bit much, even for us."

I smile until it hurts. It really does. My chest and face ache from the effort of looking delighted. I appreciate her buying these things, wanting so much to amuse me, but the cumulative effect is exhausting. How can I tell her that I've seen it all before?

That I wish we could start over with something fresh, or maybe close our eyes and relax for just one moment.

The church windows are dark tonight; rain pocks my three windows. We're both a little drunk, surrounded by torn gift wrap, caviar-smeared plates, champagne flutes cloudy with fingerprints. Vikki Carr is singing "It Must Be Him" on a CD of sixties hits a boyfriend brought as a joke then left behind.

"It's hard to believe that anybody ever took this song seriously," I say.

"It was a different world, back then. I sure don't miss it. Or your father, for that matter. I'm not bitter, that's just how it worked out." She sticks a purple adhesive bow over her ear, aiming, I guess, for a Billie Holiday nonchalance. When she pushes back her hair, I see that the red is streaked with white. "Do you ever talk to him?" she asks.

"Christmas cards, birthday cards. Not the last few years though, so I guess that's that."

"We were too young, but back then you married your mistakes. You're lucky."

Lucky. There's a concept. I can't help remembering that the guy who gave me the sixties CD, an alternative newspaper editor, broke up with me because I'd misspelled "exhilaration" and "exaltation." I hadn't even been writing about him.

It was the only time I'd ever written down a day—the only day I ever thought I needed to remember.

Just a few months ago: Things began inconsequentially enough, with a Fourth of July party at my boss Diane's house. Her husband had left her with a five-year-old boy and a bull terrier, and she was trying to make the best of it. She bought a gas grill and invited the whole office to her house in the suburbs. It was a good idea but a terrible party. The grill sputtered, the house echoed, the dog was a leg-humper, and the little boy refused to wear his pants.

Most of us were unused to children and the suburbs. We loitered under the maple trees, out of context, pretending we were pleased to see each other on the weekend. "Oh, Joy!" exclaimed my cubicle neighbor, Craig, drawling with sarcastic delight as he always does when he sees me. He likes to pun and wear amusing socks. Not everyone finds him tiresome.

At one point Roscoe, the bull terrier, leapt upon Craig's leg and led him on a panting dance across the lawn, refusing to let go until someone waved a distracting piece of steak. As the dog scampered off with the meat, Craig smoothed his chinos and addressed him with Shakespearean flourish: "Pity poor Roscoe, the product of a broken home."

"That's not funny," I said.

Craig sighed. "Oh, Joy."

"Well, it's not." Diane's little boy was right there. Oblivious, lost in nude cartwheels, but still.

I left after that, upset and embarrassed. *That's not funny.* What was happening to me? I got on the wrong highway back to the city and ended up caught in ten miles of funereally slow traffic. We all seemed to be moving in procession under the gray sky. The sky was the worst thing: low, dim, vague, unchanging. I looked at the other drivers. They weren't frowning, but they weren't smiling, either. There was neither anger nor hope, just weary acceptance, of the traffic, the weather, the steady grind of time. Adulthood, that's where I was.

I pulled off at the next rest area and walked around the picnic tables, trying to feel like my old self, the woman with the voodoo dolls, go-go boots, and inflatable Scream. I drank a high-caffeine soda, put on Fawn Fatale lipstick, and craned my throat in the rearview mirror, looking not that bad, all things considered. But I had no choice. Eventually, I had to get back on the highway. When I got home, I tried to write it all down, in the Mary Tyler Moore date book my mother had given me for Christmas.

When that prying former boyfriend was checking my spelling, he failed to notice that both "exhilaration" and "exaltation" had been preceded by the word "no."

I don't miss him. I'm not bitter, either.

My mother hands me one more present. "Something special for a special birthday."

The box is light and flat, and my mind flames up with possibilities: airline tickets, stock certificates, a cashier's check folded inside a note thanking me for being me. Gently, I remove the troll-doll wrapping paper and push the tissue aside.

It's a set of *Scream* pillowcases. Not the usual Scream-on-a-bridge but an extreme close-up. The tortured pink face is easily as large as my own.

"You don't like them."

"Mom, I do." Although, this big, the face is not nearly as lovable as it is on my dresser doll. It howls its misery right at me through full-scale lips.

"No, I can see you don't. Is it because you don't—because there's no one—" She gestures at abdomen level, making me laugh sincerely for the first time in an hour.

"Because I sleep alone? No."

"But something's wrong."

"Mom." I speak carefully. "I'm not sure I live the Scream lifestyle anymore."

"Oh. My. Well." Clearly at a loss, she looks around the room, at the electric log and unstainable carpet. "Why did you stop?"

"I didn't do it on purpose, it just happened. Things weren't so funny anymore, or maybe I just stopped wanting to laugh at them. I'm sorry."

"You certainly don't have to be sorry. If you've grown up, you've grown up, that's all."

"Is that what happened?"

"I don't know how else to explain it."

We sit like that for a moment, silent and sad, then the room fills with the throbbing, meaty voice of Tom Jones. "She's a Lady," he sings, and I begin to giggle like a junior-high kid. My mother responds with a fusillade of snorts, jumps up, and runs knock-kneed into the bathroom.

When she comes back, her eyelids are red. She sits for a long time watching the church, one thin hand clamped over her chin. "I love to laugh," she finally says. "But, you know, sometimes it's not so easy."

∞

Remorseful, I sleep that night on the *Scream* pillowcases, just so I can tell her how comfortable they are. But it's an awful night. The pillowcases crunch whenever I move. Somehow they're both scratchy and slick. And when I look in the mirror the next morning, I see that the fabric dye has bled. My face is bright pink splotched with green. Add my slicked-back hair and astonished expression, and the resemblance is unmistakable.

I don't wash my face. I wait for my mother to get up and complete her morning toilette, half an hour of splashing, brushing, and deep, deep sighs. When she finally appears, wearing, among other things, question-mark earrings and zodiac tights, she finds me sitting in the breakfast nook with my hands clamped to my temples and my mouth stretched wide in horror.

She doesn't laugh or even smile, she just stands there, taking me in. And suddenly I'm not being funny. My jaw locks open. My palms press hard against my skull. "Look, Mom." The words come out slurred; I can't move my mouth.

"I see you," she whispers. Cautiously, she touches my cheek. "Does it hurt?"

"Yes." My muscles have pulled tight over my bones; my joints have rusted in place. It feels like thirty-five years pressing in.

"All right. Joy. Listen." She puts her face close to mine and speaks loudly, as if there is a great distance between us. "Do you remember what we used to do when this happened?"

"Yes." My own strangled voice frightens me.

"I can't pick you up and carry you anymore." She sits down next to me, and I notice for the first time that my breakfast nook isn't big enough for two. "I'm not sure what to do. I didn't know this still happened."

"It doesn't." Duthn't.

"You used to snap out of it once you'd gotten my attention."

"That wuthn't it." I sound like a baby or a stroke victim. I give up talking, tears in my eyes. But it wasn't!

"It's all right, I never minded." She pats my stained face and gets up.

I want to shriek with frustration. I want to shatter into ten thousand splinters. All I can do is sit there, staring at the digital clock on the kitchenette wall. Every so often my mother leans into my field of vision to ask, "Is it getting any better?" She makes coffee, trying to hum. She's scared.

How could I have enjoyed this, feeling so helpless? But I wasn't helpless, back then. I was in control, in the center of things, making them stop for me. Now the center is somewhere else, and I'm just being carried along, a twig, a doll, a scrap. The clock clicks off its minutes, silent, ice-blue. Down on the street a crazy man is shouting, something about lost little bastards, and I can't not listen.

My arm muscles burn. My temples ache between my hard-pressing palms. Finally, my mother says, "I can't take this any more," and I expect her to call 911, but instead she goes into the bathroom for a hot washcloth. She begins to scrub my face, a little roughly, like in the old days, not caring that it hurts, preparing me for the world.

"I used to think this was growing pains. Dr. Collier said it was just a phase, those were his exact words." My real mother is back, with her worried lips and exasperated coffee breath. How good it is to see her again! To be happily dragged back home. I close my eyes against the question-mark earrings and constellation tights. Surely now the spell will break, I will be freed, but it doesn't, I'm still stopped.

"'Just a phase.' What a ridiculous explanation, and I accepted it." The washcloth pushes and scours. "We believed doctors, back then. I'd like to call Dr. Collier right now, I'd like to tell him just how wrong he was. . . . but of course he's long gone."

"Long gone." That's easy to say, even with a locked jaw.

I picture Dr. Collier hurtling down the highway, tied to the front of our gleaming old Buick. His golden hair is blowing off his head like dead grass, his handsome face is burning down to nothing. I'm there too, in the next lane, speeding like all the other drivers. I want to pull over, but my brakes don't work. Neither does the accelerator. Everyone else has the same problem. There's no way to get off the road. There's nothing to do but steer and try not to crash.

Then I realize I'm grinding my teeth.

"Mom." Only my jaw has loosened, but I sound like my real self, enough to make her put down the washcloth.

Her anxious face drops away, quickly, like a sped-past high-way sign, and although I hate to see it go—who will worry about me now?—I'm happy to be moving. My shoulders, my neck, my arms; they're sore (they're thirty-five), but at least they work.

"Get up," my mother says. "Walk around."

The kitchenette is too small. So's the living room. We have to go outside, down five flights, step by step; she won't let me take the elevator. We walk past the church and the peanut-butter cafe and a museum gift shop, at which she barely glances. She walks me all the way to the river, where the street finally dead-ends at a high cyclone fence covered with blown leaves and plastic bags. She says, "I really don't think you should stop yet. You don't want it to happen again."

"It won't happen again."

"How do you know?"

"Because I'll keep moving."

She leans against the fence, breathless from the pace she's set for me. "Maybe I should stay?" Question marks and constella-tions, her hair part-red, part-white.

"You should go."

"How can I enjoy India, worrying about you stuck in that apartment like . . ." Fighting a smile, she gropes for the funniest image. "Like a totem pole, or Charlie McCarthy, or poor old Venus de Milo."

"Mom." I have to laugh. "I can take it from here. What choice do I have? Go. *Go.*"

"Joy, are you sure? This might just be a phase."

"I know you'll give him a good home."

"I do have the perfect place for *her*, right next to the phone in the den."

"OK then." We're standing in the downstairs lobby, waiting for her cab to the airport. As Clyde the doorman pretends not to stare, I inflate Scream a final time and hand him to my mother. I expect her to stuff the doll in her new green suitcase, but she chooses to cradle it in the crook of her arm. Clyde clears his throat.

"In the meantime," she says, "I'll give her the grand tour."

"Mom!"

"Why not? Vincent will get a kick out of her. And if I leave her home, she'll run out of air completely. How do you feel?"

"Sore." The cab is pulling up at the curb.

"Bad sore?"

"Just regular."

"All right, then."

We stand close, staring, trying to take each other in, riding time, just for a moment, until there's nothing left to do but surrender: sigh and embrace, and sigh.

My mother breaks away first. She holds up Scream. "Say good-bye, dear."

"Who are you talking to?"

She laughs, and laughs.

She says, "Good-bye."

About the Author

Photo by Tim Schreiner

Ruth Hamel's stories have appeared in many magazines, including *The Kenyon Review, North American Review,* and *Missouri Review.* Her work has been nominated for a Pushcart Prize and cited in the O. Henry Awards. She lives in Connecticut.